Book One of The Dark Angel series

COURTNEY LILLARD

INFUSIONMEDIA

Lincoln, Nebraska

Infusionmedia

2124 Y St #138

Lincoln, NE 68503

https://infusion.media

Printed in the United States of America

ISBN: 978-1-945834-18-9

Library of Congress Control Number: 2020916260

Cover illustration by Isaiah McVay

instagram.com/realboyillustrations

This book is dedicated to everyone who contributed some fraction of their time to help shape the person I am today, including my parents, siblings, friends, teachers, and colleagues from across the country. I also must thank my husband, Darren, who not only gave me the push I needed to begin writing seriously and reads all of the drafts but who also listens to my ideas with honest, eager ears.

CONTENTS

1

Against the setting sun spreading over the town of Nesten, the silhouette of a child moved quickly down the dirt path and into the trees beyond. Paulina Galdwin stood in the doorway of her simple home while Coura ventured out into the woods surrounding the quiet town.

"Don't travel too far now. Supper is almost ready and it's getting dark!"

Although Coura heard her mother's voice, she continued to wander farther into the forest while waving carelessly to show she heard the call. *It's not like I haven't been lost before,* she thought absently.

Once away from the area, she burst into a full sprint, allowing her lungs to get some exercise along with her legs. Soon enough, Coura recognized her goal, a fallen tree split at the roots. In fact, it was the largest tree she had ever seen, spanning at least three times her arms' length, making it the perfect landmark in the woods outside her home.

Her pace naturally slowed to a walk after climbing over the giant log, as it always did when she passed this area. In another few minutes, she would be at her destination, the place her village labeled "Sunrise Hill." Despite the name, Coura and both of her parents found it to be the perfect area to watch the sunset as well since the sky above it opened up to both ends of the world, allowing for sunlight to pass over constantly on a clear day.

"I'll be just in time," she muttered to herself with a familiar eagerness between breaths and a quick glance up to the blue pieces of sky visible beyond the canopy.

Within a few seconds, Coura pushed through a wall of needled branches, winced as they poked her bare arms, and blinked in the sunlight pouring over the hill that overlooked miles of dense forest below. As she took a seat at the edge of the hill, the bottom of the sun's circle began to just touch the end of the earth. Coura let out a contented sigh before she relaxed and listened to the sounds of small birds, insects, and other woodland creatures shifting around. Soon enough the sky transformed into shades of orange, red, and yellow melding together against the blue that darkened over the distance away from the white sun. It was a beautiful sight at the end of the long summer months. All was at peace, something difficult to find outside of Nesten.

It's a shame only very few of us aren't afraid of what hides in the forest, she thought glumly.

In the town where Coura and her mother lived, everyone knew it to be safer during the day and within Nesten's limits. No one ventured off the trails and into the trees unless necessary and armed. Even now a short knife hung at Coura's waist, the weapon she rarely carried with her otherwise. Absolutely no one was allowed out after dark with the monstrous creatures that wandered about. She had only seen them a handful of times, and thankfully, all but one were from a great distance. Unfortunately, that encounter was the most recent, injuring the man who trained her how to hunt and fight with a knife and terrifying her for weeks.

Before that, I didn't know how dangerous they could be. Most of the other times were on this hill with Mother and Father, and we watched them walk around.

2

The creatures were difficult to make out in the shadows as their elongated bodies appeared to be covered with slick, black fur. Her father once told her that no two were alike, that some could look like giant dogs or cats, while others were more lizard-like. What he made sure she knew was that all of the creatures had purple eyes with sense in them. Before Coura could ask what he meant, her father scooped up her tiny body in his arms and the pair hurried back to Nesten.

The memory helped her remember the brief amount of time she had to return home before night fell, and with one last glance at the nearly sunken sun, Coura made her way through the brush just as the last light started to fade. The giant fallen tree was within sight when hurrying became more difficult as darkness approached. Within minutes, the woods would be pitch-black as the treetops blocked out the moon and stars.

Despite the dangers the woods brought, Coura never felt afraid. It helped that she knew how to defend herself and, most importantly, at least according to her parents, stay calm.

"As long as you remain alert and relaxed, you can prepare for whatever comes," her hunting teacher Gordon always said.

Coura smirked at the man's voice replaying in her mind. *I might not be as sharp as him,* yet, *but sometimes I wonder if everyone might be worrying over nothing. No one goes looking for trouble, so why should we all not do something to keep them away? Father never seemed too concerned when he was here.* An expected tightness gripped her heart at the thought as she put a hand on the trunk and prepared to climb over.

"It's a little dark to be wandering around, young one," said a smooth voice to Coura's right. At once, all of her muscles tensed, and she sprang back to face the stranger with knife drawn.

What? How come I didn't hear or see anyone? Coura thought frantically as she scrambled to stand how Gordon taught her when defending. She spread her feet wide while leaning forward a bit and keeping her arms apart as if expecting the stranger to attack. Instead, the woman in front of her laughed sweetly and stepped closer.

"Oh, calm down," the stranger said with a finger pointing at the knife. "Put that toy away now, I only want to talk for a moment."

Although it was dark, Coura could tell this woman wasn't human, at least not entirely. Black, silky hair flowed down like a wave to her waist, something Coura felt her mother would scoff at, and her skin-tight outfit covered all but the face, hands, and feet. Three aspects of this creature immediately convinced Coura she was not human. Firstly, her eyes were a deep violet with humor dancing in them, then she noticed the tips of two pointed ears sticking out from the woman's hair. Finally, and most frightening, was her charming smile while approaching Coura with sharp canine teeth. The realization made her knees shake.

I've never seen a shadow creature take a human form, but this woman doesn't exactly feel *human at all either. Is she something entirely new?* she wondered while still remaining solid despite her fear.

This time, the woman waved her hand at the knife with amusement. "I told you already, I just want to talk, child."

"If you don't mind, I would rather be on my way," Coura countered in a weak voice. Slowly, she backed up a pace to prepare to go around the trunk still blocking her way home.

"You're from that town near here, aren't you?" the enchantingly smooth voice asked with interest.

The stranger startled her by circling the fallen tree swiftly to stand in front of Coura's path like a leaf dancing in the wind. Sweat began to trickle down Coura's neck as she saw how fast the woman moved, and how it would be impossible to escape by running. Somehow, she managed to speak somewhat calmly once more, though the words seemed to pour out while her mind raced for an excuse to get away.

"Who are you? We shouldn't stay out here after dark or else the monsters in these woods will come after us. If you're looking for something, I can help direct you to the nearest road."

The woman's eyes narrowed slightly, then she looked in the direction of Nesten. "Do not fret, dear one, I already found what I desire." Her tone suggested that something unpleasant awaited the people in Coura's hometown.

As they stood in the silence that followed, Coura's hopes sank and her body grew so tense that her head throbbed. Never before did she see herself in this kind of danger, the one where fighting to escape was not an option, and most likely not only her life was on the line. Finally, the woman crossed her arms, tilted her head, and addressed Coura once more.

"You're all alone," she said coolly, focusing on Coura's vulnerability. "I can sense the beings around here, but even so, I've visited this area quite enough to know you humans fear the creatures at night. Yet, for some reason, you chose to come out here." A wide grin graced her lips full of mischief. "Lucky me."

Even though she was practically paralyzed with fear like a small animal, Coura became hypnotized by the woman's voice. Her gentle tone lulled Coura into a near trance, keeping her hanging on every word. It became difficult just to think.

"I have an idea," the stranger continued with a finger on her lip, seemingly oblivious to Coura's fears and internal struggle.

"You see, I am very bored. I think I can have some fun with you. What's your name, young one?"

"Coura," she responded automatically, still unable to process the situation. *What's going on? This isn't like any creature I've seen or heard about. She can't be human, can she? What does she mean by "having fun" with me?*

"Ah... *Coura*," the woman said, stretching the name as if tasting it like the adults did with wines and ciders. "What a lovely name."

Coura couldn't even flinch as the stranger put one hand under her chin and tilted it up so their eyes met. Only then could she see that what she thought were the woman's clothes was really a part of her skin, like a smooth fur. The sleek, fit body beneath could not distract her from the muscles underneath. Her breath caught at the stranger's next words.

"You see, dear one, I am a demon. You may call me Soirée."

She let out a giggle as Coura felt her eyes widen with sheer terror. *A demon? This can't be real, can it? They were only in stories about the founding of Asteom, so how is she here?*

Only whispers of demons ever reached the children in Nesten, mostly because no one knew anyone who had ever seen or heard of one besides in the story of their country's creation. For one thing, they were remote and spent their days alone seeking power and causing pain and trouble. For another, they fought with the angelic beings who protected the humans in Asteom by chasing demons away. However, the angels eventually had become as scarce as demons. There was one other piece of information Coura was familiar with regarding demons.

They possess people. They take over their bodies and destroy their minds. That's why we never hear about them—everyone who was in contact with them gets killed! Wait, she said she wanted me to keep

6

her entertained. Does that mean ... I'm only a child. What could she possibly use a child for?

While all of this ran through Coura's mind, the creature, Soirée, continued to smile down at her. Something else, an anger and annoyance at her situation, began mixing in with the fear. "What do you want?" she choked out, but succeeded in showing that hint of frustration.

Sadly, it was a pathetic gesture that only made the demon chuckle again. "Why such hostility? I said I want to have fun, and because I am so generous, you get to share in it too! What do you think? Will you let me borrow your body for a while?"

"It's not like I have a choice." Coura couldn't stop herself from mumbling, which the creature heard and laughed at. By now, her chest hurt from the strain of the pounding heartbeats while her knees threatened to give out. All she wanted to do was cry.

I'm just a child. Why would she do this? It has to be a nightmare... I wish Mother were here, or Father, or Gordon.

At the thought of her family and hometown, Coura grew curious about the demon's intentions. She couldn't help herself from glancing up into the creature's face and noting a patient expression. *Does she expect me to respond? I might as well give up now. If she wants to capture me, I have a feeling I wouldn't even know what happened. Why does she hesitate? Could it really all be for her own sick entertainment to torture me and the other townsfolk?*

Something about this encounter didn't sit right with Coura, about being caught alone on a regular trek away from Nesten. No matter what, she knew in her aching heart that the demon would not let her go. *If that is the case, I can't willingly let her hurt Mother and the others in town.*

"You are ... asking me, right?" Coura said calmer than she felt.

"I suppose I am, child," Soirée responded lazily, as if the waiting was growing tiresome.

"Do demons keep promises?"

The demon tilted her head curiously like an animal and raised an eyebrow. "A demon never lies. At least, I don't."

Coura swallowed and sheathed her knife against her protesting instincts. For her idea to work, she had to believe Soirée. "If all you want is something to entertain yourself, I will help under one condition."

The demon didn't even try to hide her amusement. "Oh? I'm quite interested in hearing this."

All at once, the inevitability of her fate caught up with Coura. A single tear escaped her watering eyes while her lips quivered. *After all*, she repeated in her mind, *I'm only a child. I shouldn't die so soon and all alone.*

"I would like to make a deal with you..."

* * *

Byron Rinod leaned forward with a recently lit torch to squint at a nearby forest in the opposite direction he was heading. Something felt wrong, something only a mage like himself could sense, and that worried him considerably. Quickly, Byron glanced around as he backtracked his steps until he found a path leading in that direction and made haste.

That was a dark magic spell if I ever knew one, but I don't remember feeling such a surge of power from this great a distance before. Something else is there too... Could it be a demonic creature?

With that consideration in mind, Byron hurried his pace down the worn path. Thankfully, it was clear so he could do so without the possibility of running into someone else.

Yes, it must be from one, he continued thinking with more certainty as the energies grew nearer. *Only a demonic creature has that type of unnatural power. At least I know I didn't come all this way for nothing, even though I truly wish for everything to be all right.*

As a master mage, it was his responsibility to address any harmful situations that involved dark energies stemming from humans or demonic creatures, or worse. He spotted a cloud of gray smoke hovering against the starry, moonless sky with a sinking feeling before racking his brain for the possibilities.

I'm not terribly familiar with the eastern part of these woods, but if I recall correctly, they are mostly small towns, meaning none of our mages should be posted there. That leaves me dealing with either someone new to using their magic, a demonic creature, or a ritual to summon a demon. I doubt our scouts would have missed a person with such great power instead of taking them to the academy for training. Besides, I can sense the wrongness of a demon's energies at work and, with the increase in creatures, I must assume the worst.

His eleven years of training and teaching magic users at the Magic Arts Academy provided him with plenty of experience in dealing with various levels of dark and light energies, although he was skilled in the former. Even so, Byron was not entirely familiar with this area and noted the unnatural silence lingering like the increasing smoke and burning scent.

In a short amount of time, he approached the entrance to the town marked by a pair of stone buildings on either side of the road, wide enough for two carts to pass through side by side. A haunting glow came from beyond that, indicating fire. Still, Byron made sure not to rush in as there was always the possibility of an ambush from the source.

I don't sense any magical energies, and it appears all of the townsfolk are gone. What that implied could not be determined by standing at a distance. He relaxed a bit, then continued walking.

There were several more stone structures that appeared to have been shops with houses made of brick and clay scattered in between. Most of the glass windows were broken inward, any roofs made of straw were dwindling beneath dying flames, and the sides of all of the structures had scorch marks. Inside the homes, only a few pieces of furniture were on fire, which intrigued Byron. From all that he observed as he made his way to the remaining buildings, there were no bodies and no burning-flesh stench that usually meant the worst.

If the person or creature responsible was not out to destroy everything, raid the empty homes, or kill at first sight, why would they be here in the first place? I still don't sense any energies, so unless they can somehow hide from me, I should be clear.

He glanced up and down the final rows, thankful that the entire town was only made up of about thirty businesses and homes. At last, he reached the edge and turned around with a sigh.

There's nothing left under my jurisdiction to investigate. If I can't sense anything, the mage or creature must be long gone by now, Byron thought with dismay. *I'll have to make my way back to the MAA and send a scout to this place in the morning. It's a shame we don't have enough students to send to these smaller towns. In most cases, they could use the protection more than the cities.*

Suddenly, Byron felt a weak brush on his mind signaling the presence of magic. The sensation was fairly indescribable, but when he needed to explain it to those young students who were unfamiliar with it, he told them to imagine someone "tickling" their brain. It was near enough to the truth and lighthearted so that they often laughed at his outrageousness. With how faintly most mages could sense energies, it got the point across. Only a powerful mage like himself could sense magic at a distance and distinguish certain features, like if it was considered light or dark.

Byron quickly tracked the energies back to the middle of the town and behind the first two homes. He nearly overlooked the small figure crumpled up in the shadows, but the trail led him there. Carefully, he knelt beside the body of a girl he thought no older than twelve and put a hand on her arm. It was cold and trembling. When she didn't respond to his touch, Byron decided to brush away the black hair covering her face and check for breathing. The child was alive but suffering from some sort of shock. He knew exactly what this meant.

She isn't hurt and the energies stem from her, which means something triggered the power. It makes sense; after all, a lot of mages discover their magic around this age and without warning.

"Hello, is anyone around here?" he called toward the main path while rising. "I am a master mage from the Magic Arts Academy in East Hoover. The danger has passed, but I need to speak with someone." Only the crackling of the many dying flames answered.

Byron swore under his breath and tried to figure out what to do. *A whole town disappears and leaves a child behind. They were probably afraid of her potential, which I must admit is great if it caused all of this. I can feel the dark energies stirring, but they seem normal compared to what I felt before. Could there have been a demonic creature who startled her into using magic?*

As he looked down once more at the girl, Byron wiped his sweaty forehead and thought about what he should do next.

According to the MAA's policy, anyone with demon or angelic blood, and thus the ability to wield dark or light magic, was to be taken in by the academy to foster their growing energies. This was both for the safety of the individual as well as those around them who were vulnerable to untrained abilities.

This isn't the first time an inexperienced magic user caused damage to their home or frightened their family away. Usually I would need permission from the child's guardian to help. However, I cannot in good conscience let her stay here or go on without training. Her destructive potential must be reined in as soon as possible, even if it means leaving things as they are at the moment.

By now it was well into the night, and Byron was exhausted from the full day of travel, meaning there was no use in trying to get to East Hoover before morning. He pulled off the packs he still carried on his shoulders and set everything up in the middle of the town for a makeshift camp.

At least I won't freeze to death, he thought bitterly, watching the fires go out on their own and the smoke continue to rise instead of crowd the town. *On a more positive note, if anyone returns or comes to help, we will be here to explain the situation, and I can let them know I'll be taking her. It shouldn't be any trouble that way.*

After setting up his own bedroll and placing an extra blanket next to it in the dirt, Byron brought the limp body over and laid the girl down on it while politely taking the blanket for himself. He was used to sleeping outdoors on the ground by now. His last thought before sleep took him was that the area would be safe to venture on in the morning, meaning the townsfolk would eventually return. To his dismay, when Byron rose at the first sign of light, he and the girl were still alone. After waiting until midmorning in the hope of seeing someone, Byron decided it would be best to move on with the still unconscious girl.

When I get the chance, I will have to return here or send a messenger to relay the news and her status. Hopefully, by then there will be survivors who can confirm my suspicions about what took place here last night.

2

Coura stood with her back to the metal door of the spacious, circular workspace that served as the classroom. The stone room held little furniture, only an empty wooden chair and table at one end for the instructor, who was currently tending to a call from some other teacher. Because of the lack of anything else, the area could hold her entire dark magics class, consisting of Coura and twelve other mages in training with a ring in the center for combat demonstrations and shielding practice. At the moment, she seized the opportunity to demonstrate her own abilities to the rest of the class, but mostly for two students in particular.

Joshua and Selma always brag about their control over a fire spell, but I think their opinions will change once they see mine. Master Leni picked the perfect time to leave for a while, Coura thought to herself with a smile at what she prepared to do.

After taking a deep breath, Coura extended her right arm with the palm out at the other end of the room and focused on the dark energies humming in her center. Four years of training with Byron, who she saw as the top mage at the academy, made spells easy to learn. In fact, she had been told multiple times over the years that she was the strongest trainee among her peers—just not by them.

I think I would be jealous too if another classmate were so far above me, she thought with a touch of vanity. *After all, I'm the only student Byron has worked with individually for so long.*

"Well, what are you waiting for?" the rosy-cheeked girl named Selma asked in an impatient tone while standing off to the side in front of their other classmates.

Joshua, the tall, lean boy at her side, bobbed his head twice. "Master Leni will be back soon if you don't hurry."

"If you would shut up, I could concentrate," Coura mumbled loud enough for them to hear, then tapped into the energies within herself. Casting a spell was like releasing a dam holding the power in her center. Once it was triggered, the user would need to lead the energies to their hands and manifest the spell, otherwise that power would find another way to exit that was often painful and uncontrolled. With her years of practice, this took less than a moment for Coura to achieve with only a bit of recoil after releasing the spell.

"Manifesting a spell simply requires you to pull forth your own energy and command it to take the physical form of something, say fire, lightning, or a shielding wall. A mage's responsibility is to control the power within themselves along with that around them. Without control, they destroy their body and soul while tampering with the natural energies around us." Byron sure hammered that into my head during my first year.

From her hand shot out a bright red fireball as big as a melon that exploded into flames once it connected with the cool, stone wall opposite from where she stood. There were small gasps from some of the students, but most waited eagerly for more. Just as the sparks from the previous spell touched the ground, Coura launched two more blasts in the exact same spot. The room fell silent. She turned with a smirk knowing that was difficult for most mages to accomplish, but still Joshua, Selma, and a few others gave her unimpressed looks.

This time, she was determined to silence their doubts about her, even if it meant extending the display a bit longer. The wooden chair that had been pulled away from the table when Master Leni exited appeared tempting enough. With another reach into her center pool of energies, Coura swiped her hand across the air, releasing a straight shot of flames directed to her target. The chair rocked back from the blow but didn't fall over. Instead, it became covered with the flames and charred beneath them.

Only when she remembered that they were in a sealed room, leaving no opening for the smoke, did she expend more energy, this time in the form of an ice spell. The crystals were released in such a unique way that they joined together to form a snow-like blast of air. Not only was the chair saved from burning up, but it became covered in a thin layer of frost that would soon melt.

Coura prepared to face her fellow trainees once more and gloat when the door to the training space opened. Every student jumped at the sound before turning with wide eyes to see Master Leni frozen in the doorway, an expression of surprise written on her face, then replaced with a rage Coura recognized only too well.

"What is going on here?" their instructor's shrill voice asked as she walked in without closing the door.

Of course, no one spoke up. If they thought Coura would, they should have thought better. She had been caught in this type of situation often enough to know that Master Leni wouldn't listen as she reprimanded disobedience.

The instructor's eyes went straight to Coura, who stood alone in the center of the room and lowered her head at the expected punishment.

"I should have known," Master Leni said, biting off the end of each word in disgust. "Everyone, we will pick up with this tomorrow. I expect better behavior from all of you then!"

The older woman watched the class exit like a hawk. Her skinny build and long face were made more menacing with her graying hair pulled up into a tight bun at the top of her head. Each trainee kept their head down and silently hurried away before they drew her wrath. Only Coura remained where she was, knowing a lecture was coming, and possibly worse from her past troubles. Once alone, Master Leni slowly closed the door and let out a frustrated sigh.

"This is the fourth time this year, Coura," she began and held out her hands in a plea. "I don't understand why we keep having this issue."

She waited for some sort of reply and scowled when Coura didn't give one. *Of course she's upset. Anything I tell her wouldn't be good enough. I can't tell her I'm bored in this group again or she will tell me to find something else to keep my mind occupied outside of class. If I mention how far above the other students I am again, she would just yell at me for "overstating my abilities."*

Master Leni had no tolerance for anything not under her control and supervision, which meant she and Coura didn't get along. After a few more seconds under that scowl, Coura watched the instructor as she gestured for Coura to follow her out into the hall. They both knew the way to the headmaster's office, so the master mage made no effort to keep track of her. Master Leni was certainly not the only instructor who felt it necessary to send Coura there.

She ignored the curious glances of the many students scattered around the academy halls at this break in the afternoon classes. Too many seemed to shoot her expressions as if saying,

"Coura's in trouble again? What a surprise," while they snickered behind her back. Their reactions never really bothered her, though, as they knew nothing of the real issue bringing about her misbehavior. They soon approached the office and, without a word, slipped inside.

Headmaster Symon's main office was past a waiting area where his secretary, named Jann, worked at a desk covered with stacks of paperwork. A window behind Jann's desk let in plenty of light, and Coura wished she would open it to let some fresh air into the stuffy room. The woman sat upright at the sound of their arrival and finished what she was writing but relaxed a trifle when she saw who had entered.

"Master Leni, good afternoon to you," Jann greeted the instructor with a genuine smile. Coura's teacher acknowledged it with a sharp nod.

"Same to you. Is the headmaster in?"

"Yes, ma'am," Jann replied and gestured to the door on her right. "You can head on in."

Master Leni glanced over at Coura, who had already taken a seat in one of two wobbly chairs against the wall farthest from the headmaster's room. "I expect you to remain here and not cause trouble for Jann!"

Coura sat upright and gave a mock salute as the woman turned and basically stormed in to see Headmaster Symon.

"Oh, Master Leni! I wasn't expecting you," she heard the headmaster say, then the door was closed and only soft murmurs were audible. Coura relaxed and let out a quiet groan of displeasure. Jann gave her a sympathetic look, then went back to her business. Although the two crossed paths often enough, Jann was always working on something and never felt the need to make conversation.

Then again, what could you say to someone in trouble, Coura wondered as she waited. *I just wish this didn't warrant a visit to the headmaster. Do they think they can't say anything to me directly besides scolding my behavior? What do they worry I will do when I leave this place?* That thought took her mind in another direction.

The entire academy basically taught three types of students until the age of sixteen: scholars, soldiers, and mages. Most scholars consisted of the children of nobles, craftsmen, merchants, or other families whose children showed high enough skills in reading, writing, geography, and history. There were not very many of these students, for the well-off could afford tutors or schools closer to the capital city of Verona and merchants and craftsmen could apprentice them instead.

Other children who were not destined for inheriting a position within a family business or who preferred physical work, an honorable title, and serving the country went into the army. Coura had heard that some families in cities considered it a tradition to have at least one child in their generation bring glory to their name. The basics of fighting with a variety of weapons was taught before the trainees were sent off in graduating classes to join Verona's armies. About a dozen students left every spring, so that option was fairly common in this area.

The remaining students were magic users with the potential to become mages. Most of the MAA consisted of mage trainees as this was the one place to be trained outside of the palace in the capital city. Graduating mages were given four options once they prepared to leave as their skills often varied.

Those with the intellect and patience or who were too old or injured to do much else could stay or return at a later time to teach future mages. Others with the skills were encouraged to serve in the army. All students at the academy were taught how to wield a weapon, whether it be for defending or attacking. Another option, and the most common, was to be stationed as a guard for cities and towns. There, they worked alongside posted soldiers to protect and keep peace. Students who favored staying close to home or who, more often than not, were not physically or emotionally fit enough to handle combat chose this path. The final option was for individuals who showed special talents useful to the king, generals, and master mages in the palace. Not too many people were recommended for these positions since there were so few, including spies, assassins, ambassadors, and other unique jobs, but the trainees all knew there was a chance.

By the time a student turned sixteen and graduated, they had some inclination as to what they were going to do. Both dark and light mages were necessary in any position, so a trainee was able to really do whatever their heart was set on.

Unfortunately, Coura had no notion of what she wanted her future to be. *Because I grew up here, surrounded by combat and magic, I don't have a home or a family to influence my decision. I think it would be boring to stay in one place for years, and I doubt anyone in the academy would vouch for me to teach even if I wanted to. That leaves the army, which I could tolerate if I had to, but even the thought of taking orders from a stranger bothers me. But if I had to choose, that would probably be the best fit for me.*

The more she thought about the decision, the more uncertain she felt. What was worse, she was one of the oldest students, meaning she was due to graduate and be forced to choose. *I'm almost certain you are placed before your seventeenth birthday, whether you agree with it or not. By then, you already know what you need to learn and are only wasting space in a classroom.*

Muffled yelling from the headmaster's main office caught Coura and Jann's attention, causing them to involuntarily glance at the door.

"Symon, I don't care about policies," they heard Master Leni shout. Softer, inaudible words followed, undoubtedly from the headmaster. "...can't comply! I've never... She should be removed and ... send somewhere. It would be easier on all of us!" More mumbling and hysteric words took place before the two went quiet. Coura felt herself flush with a mixture of frustration and embarrassment when they continued once more.

Master Leni spoke in the same fashion, emphasizing Coura's abilities and lack of responsibility. At the desk, Jann coughed uncomfortably and caught her attention. The woman's cheeks were also bright red as if she didn't feel that she should be listening in.

"I'm going to run these documents over to the messenger's office," she said and stood with a handful of papers. "Please, Coura, behave while I'm away. Hopefully, it shouldn't be much longer..."

At those words, they both nearly jumped as Master Leni cried, "and another thing" before going into a rant on the placement of Coura in that particular class as opposed to another instructor who "has more time on their hands and less students in their class." Coura's impression was that Master Leni was now using this opportunity to complain about the other instructors and the drama going on with scheduling and class sizes. Jann made her exit then, pretending to ignore the headmaster's office and leaving Coura alone to unwillingly listen.

The conversation became more civil within the next minute, so Coura had to strain her ears to hear what the headmaster's verdict would be. If he was sympathetic toward her because of

Master Leni's attitude, she would get extended outside work or additional chores, punishments she was all too familiar with. However, she had no idea what his decision would be if he took no favor on her.

Coura noticed then that every other time she had been sent or escorted to his office, Headmaster Symon never directly spoke with her. There was a brief lecture on what he considered to be the duties of a mage her age, then his verdict.

He should be used to assigning my punishments, but I've never heard any of my instructors yell like that. Did I go too far by scorching the furniture? It was not the worst thing I've done, but why do I have a feeling this time was different?

Suddenly, she heard Byron's name and stretched her ears to eavesdrop. When their words were still too muffled, Coura snuck over to the door and listened with one ear against the thick wood. If Jann was going to leave her alone to avoid being involved, she probably would not return until Master Leni took her leave.

"He's shirking his responsibilities here, and we have no idea why." That was Master Leni's high-pitched voice followed by the headmaster's soothing, yet firm tone.

"I understand your frustration, but this is a private matter with the king and his council. We can't place any trainees with Byron because he is leaving again this afternoon, and every other dark magic instructor has full courses."

"He is the only one who can tolerate her misbehavior. Now that he's running back to Verona *again*, I will not stand for any more outbursts. This time it was a chair; last time she almost struck another student with a bolt of lightning while we were focused on other spells!"

Coura winced at the memory, remembering her intention to practice something more advanced that Byron started her on.

After, Master Leni immediately proceeded to recall another incident that left bruises and a long but shallow cut on another student when she chose to work with real swords instead of their wooden practice ones while the instructor was helping a new mage trainee.

What struck her the hardest was not talk of her past troubles nor the lack of places for them to move her, but the fact that her favorite, preferred teacher was leaving once more and the lack of compassion from any of her instructors. Reluctantly, Coura pushed away from the door and stood in the middle of the room, unsure of what to think.

Byron is the only one who actually cares about me, not just about obedience and potential. I never misbehave when I'm with him because of it. That, and the fact that I feel like I am making progress when I work with him and not toying around relearning the basics. I can't believe he is leaving for the capital today. Last time he was gone for two weeks, and before that he was only here for a week and a half. Another consideration came to mind then.

Last time Byron went to Verona, he avoided confronting anyone. He doesn't have many students, at least no one that needs his training like I do, so he isn't leaving much behind. Since the headmaster made it sound like the other instructors don't know about his visits, I doubt Byron makes an effort to tell anyone besides Headmaster Symon.

Coura glanced around the empty office as she wondered what to do. *I think Jann will be taking her time, and there are too many eyes in the hallway outside. Byron might be in his room. If I can speak with him before he leaves, maybe he can give me some advice against Master Leni and the other instructors. In any case, I really don't feel like listening to another lecture on responsibility.*

* * *

Headmaster Symon held his tongue while his subordinate continued venting about her student, Master Byron, and the other instructors' inability to cooperate and communicate with one another. Beneath the annoyance at her overly dramatic tone, he was genuinely interested in what Leni was saying.

I can't believe Byron doesn't share with them what he has been working on. The fool. Now I am the one who has to deal with the mages' backlash, he thought ruefully.

In truth, it was better for Byron to avoid mentioning why he was making the frequent trips to the palace in the capital city of Verona. However, Symon had not thought it would lead to suspicion and hostility among the other instructors. After all, what his friend was working on dealt with the future of graduating academy mages.

Once Leni stopped to breathe, Symon pounced on his opportunity to explain the situation. "Leni, would you like to know *why* Byron is traveling so much?"

"I suppose it's better late than never." The older woman tried to hide her interest and failed.

She is just concerned, as I hear all of the instructors are. They know something is going on under their noses. I figure I would be anxious as well, he told himself after a deep breath. Symon's ability to rationalize with a level head was one of the reasons he was recommended by his peers to take up his place as headmaster of the academy.

"You see, Byron is our strongest dark mage and has always worked with the fewest number of students. He has been to the capital for training before serving and is still young enough to travel often. Also, I personally recommended him as our representative for King Hernan's council because of his critical thinking skills and patience." Symon paused, waiting for any additional comments.

"Well, get on with it," was all Master Leni said with an edge.

"To put it plainly, Byron is constructing a contract of sorts with King Hernan and the army commanders..."

He went into detail explaining the "contract" and what both sides of it, the academy and the army, had to say. By the end, the old mage was hunched over with fingers laced across her lap. She wore a thoughtful expression, then spoke with a calmness that startled him a little.

"I see now. That explains much more than I thought."

"I am glad we had this discussion," Symon admitted while rising from his desk to conclude their meeting. His legs were becoming stiff from sitting nearly all day. "I'm going to ask you to spread this news to the other instructors and apologize on my behalf. Please advise them not to speak of this to the trainees as well. I am genuinely sorry it took this long for you to find out what is happening, but I believe it was better for all of you to hear it now while it is only a possibility."

Master Leni rose as well, visibly drained from the discussion, and nodded.

All of that ranting worn her out. The poor woman, she must have been suppressing her suspicion and uncertainty up to the boiling point. Speaking of which, we never discussed young Coura.

"I suppose I should deal with your student as well sometime today," he joked, and, to his relief, she laughed.

"Oh, Symon, I nearly forgot about her. My mind is leaving me fast lately."

"It's just making room for more important matters," he reassured her with a chuckle.

"I honestly do not know what to do with her," Leni admitted as she pinched the bridge of her nose. "What I told you from the beginning is true. I have never dealt with a student who is so determined to disobey instructions from every teacher."

The bags under her eyes told Symon she was not lying about the burden of the extra students in their classes due to Byron's absence, or their consistent troublemaker.

Every child growing into a young adult goes through a period of time where they act independent and troublesome. With that being said, I can't recall any other students who have caused this much stress on the instructors. Could it be because she has a unique past without any connections to family or her hometown?

As Symon ushered the tired woman from his office, he thought about the first time he had met Coura four years ago. Byron, of all people, was the one who brought the confused, senseless girl to him for recovery. The amount of dark energy surrounding her was enough for even a lesser mage like Symon to sense.

I don't believe the scouts we sent to Nesten found any remaining inhabitants, and they typically visit for a few days after such an event. The town is occupied now, but nothing else took place within the following four years that I've heard. Besides, from what Byron has told me Coura has no memories of the place or interest in visiting, which was why he never pursued investigating where the other townsfolk went. Such a strange turn of events that brought her to us indeed.

Of course, Byron volunteered to take the girl under his wing, giving her private tutoring to nurture her abilities that far outdistanced the other trainees her age. With no knowledge of her background in schooling, Coura was given basic exams for academics, combat skills, and magic. She grew passionate about everything except the textbook courses, such as history, geography, and mathematics, and picked up on spells as easily as breathing. This was all according to her teachers' experiences, in part, when they would speak with him, but mostly from what Byron shared in private.

"It's just that attitude of hers," his friend would complain. "She has all that potential and no interest in controlling it. She accomplishes one task, hones one ability before diving into five others without completely understanding why it is necessary to do things a certain way or take the process step by step. When I tell her to relax and focus, she becomes upset with me, arguing that our pace is too slow. If it isn't keeping her entertained, it's not worth the time, in her eyes. The worst of it all is that she learns the 'how' so quickly, faster than any of my previous students, but couldn't care less about the 'why.' If she put in the extra effort and time to do that, she would not be messing around in her classes."

I believe it was after he said that last bit that I referred to him as a "borderline parent" for Coura. With that in mind, Byron does tolerate her mischief because he understands her personality, abilities, and progress as he has been her primary teacher. Since he is traveling, though, she is unable to train properly at the same level, leading to a lack of interest in simpler classes, then unintentionally causing trouble.

Symon still had no notion as to what he could say to help Coura's situation, but at the moment he needed to provide some sort of response if only to satisfy Master Leni. He let out a long sigh, opened his office door with the woman exiting behind, and stood alone in front of his secretary's desk.

"Where is she?" he muttered to himself as he moved to the door leading out into the hallway.

"I cannot believe this," Leni exclaimed from where she stood at his side. "I give her one thing to do, a simple order, and she disappears!"

Against his own disappointment in the girl, Symon wondered how long they were conversing and peeked out into the hallway. He saw Jann leafing through a stack of papers in her hands further down, yet not out of earshot.

I bet she felt uncomfortable with the yelling. I recall that her home life involved constantly bickering relatives, so it is no problem that she needed to leave at the first sign of a verbal argument.

Symon cleared his throat, a sound that filled the nearly empty space. "Jann?"

The young lady looked up with slight relief and hurried over. "Headmaster, forgive me. I just wanted to run these to the messenger's office, but they had their own meeting and I wasn't sure how long it would take for both spaces to clear."

He put a reassuring hand on her shoulder accompanied by a smile that she returned, then led them inside. As Jann took her seat and rearranged different sheets of paper, Leni tapped a foot and crossed her arms, but said nothing. Symon noticed the gesture, curious himself if Jann saw Coura sneak out, and decided to ask. He grew concerned when she shook her head with a worried face of her own.

"I was in front of the door for a while," she started. "I would have seen if she had left."

Leni, finally out of patience for the situation, threw her hands up. "Coura couldn't have just disappeared!"

After a moment of confused silence, a warm summer breeze blew through the room. Symon closed his eyes, preparing to figure out his next words when Jann begged his pardon.

"Headmaster Symon, I am not sure what Coura made of your words, but I do know that when I left, the window was closed."

* * *

A sturdy pack filled with clothes, dried meats and other food items, and various tools and utensils lay in front of Byron, He nodded with approval at the contents. In the back of his mind, the master mage told himself not to worry as he had made the five-day trip to the capital numerous times. The servants there also knew him well enough to have extras of just about everything stored for when he arrived.

"You're leaving again?" said an irritated voice from behind that Byron had become accustomed to hearing.

A glance up from his bag showed his primary student Coura sitting on the sill of his open window with an unamused look. He matched the expression, trying to hide his disappointment at being caught heading out once again without mentioning it to anyone.

"I thought you would be in training now," he said to cover up the fact.

Coura crossed her arms and frowned. "You were planning on sneaking out of here at the busiest time of the day to avoid seeing anyone. That's very selfish of you."

When Byron didn't answer, instead closing and tying up his bag, she hopped off the windowsill and walked up to where he remained kneeling next to his things.

"You realize you are almost finished with your training, right? Skipping out on the extra practice hinders your progress."

"I already know everything in those classes," his student shrugged arrogantly without pausing. "They can't teach me what you can." Byron didn't have to ask who "they" were. Both

Coura and Symon informed him when her instructors grew impatient with her attitude, usually resulting in her being sent to the headmaster's office.

I'm only thirty-six years old, yet all of this work and these constant trips to argue with royalty are taking their toll on my body. Not to mention my own lack of training, both physically and magically. If Coura could just be patient until my business is done, or she graduates in the spring, life will become more interesting.

He sighed, rose, and reluctantly decided to face the conversation he had put aside for weeks. With as stern a look as possible, Byron took in the most powerful yet most troublesome student he had the pleasure of working with. In the four years since Coura had been brought to the academy, she had developed into a young woman, tough fighter, and unique mage. Unbound raven hair trailed down her back, blowing slightly in the gentle breeze from the window, as her eyes as blue as the sky outside shone with unfavorable emotions toward what he was doing. More than once Byron noted how rare the combination of physical characteristics was.

Typically, a mage with demon blood in their veins who can wield dark energies carries similar features to their ancestors. Black or coppery hair, pale skin sensitive to sunlight, and green eyes are key indicators. I am a pretty good example, Byron reflected while running a hand through his inky hair.

In addition to those with dark blood, meaning somewhere in time their lineage traced back to the demons that lived beneath the planet's surface, there were ordinary humans and light-blooded mages. The first humans in the country were said to have brown eyes and hair complementing their tan skin, which scholars believed was from working out in the fields. Since they were unable to manipulate magical energies, typically someone with those features was not destined to be a mage.

The other mages, those with light blood, were said to be descendants of the angelic race that lived in the hidden city of Yeluthia, otherwise known as the "city in the clouds." Hundreds of years ago, the angels protected humans from the demons, sealing the demons beneath the surface of the planet. Anyone with their power could wield light magic and typically had blond or even white hair, fair skin, and signature blue eyes. Nowadays, bloodlines were so mixed that features hardly mattered when judging whether someone will possess the ability to use magic. However, he had never met anyone with blue eyes and black hair before.

As for Byron, he appeared as one would expect with hair color matching Coura's and emerald eyes. He stood a head taller than his student, who continued watching him with interest, and was built for combat with muscular arms and a broad chest.

After the long pause while all of this came to mind, he caved in. "Why aren't you in class?"

She stood her ground, as usual. "Why are you leaving again?"

"I asked you first," he countered with a knowing grin.

"We were let out early." That was all she said, and Byron had the feeling there was more to it.

"You got yourself in trouble again, didn't you?"

A brief flash of surprise passed over her face before the indignation returned, and she hesitated before answering. "I didn't do anything wrong. I just didn't do exactly what Master Leni wanted."

Byron rubbed his weary eyes. *If I am counting this right, this is the eighth time this school year I've heard something from either her, Symon, or another instructor.*

"Coura..." he began before she cut him off.

"It's not my fault! When I'm in classes, I'm bored, Byron. You and I both know my magic is stronger than the other students'. I do what the instructors ask, but I'm wasting my time there."

"Have you *really* taken the time to learn about the spells, or just how to cast them?" he asked skeptically.

She nodded with more confidence than Byron expected. "Yes, I know how to cast the types of spells. I've practiced how much energy to put into a spell and played around with the form it takes." Coura went on to explain the situation that had put her in the headmaster's office. Despite her disobedience and the risks involved, he was proud of her progress and how the spells were manipulated.

As she neared the end, Byron deduced that there was more to Leni's reasoning for visiting Symon. *While Coura's actions were unnecessary, I wouldn't deem it horrible enough for her to visit the headmaster's office. Also, for Leni to blow up on him like that loud enough for Coura to hear is very unprofessional and uncharacteristic of the woman. I'm assuming since my name was brought up, she and the other instructors are curious as to my work in Verona. How will Symon react to this?*

Coura finished her account and appeared to be waiting for some sort of reassurance, which he was not feeling inclined to give at the moment. "Do you not trust your instructors' knowledge?"

She gave him a confused look before answering. "Well, no. They are fine, I suppose, but—"

"Did you ever stop to think that there is more to magic training than learning the spells?" he cut her off without holding back some of his own personal frustration. "They have age and experience over you and the other trainees that allows them to

33

prepare you for the future. If you bothered to practice in those classes, I can tell you, you would become more precise and exert less energy. I know I've told you that before, Coura! Your problem is that you can't see the bigger picture, the *why* of what you are taught in class. Without that, you are nothing more than a mindless worker thoughtlessly going through life."

Coura did *not* take criticism well, Byron knew that much as he saw her whole body tense up and face flush with repressed anger and shame. However, he had dealt with her enough by now to know when he was seriously pushing her limits.

Although Byron did not step down, he returned her glare and continued in a more patient tone. "Why I am telling you this is because by disobeying their instructions, you are not only flirting with potential danger to others who are less skilled but also showing your classmates it is OK for them to test their own power unsupervised and disobey orders. We've had plenty of accidents both here and out in the field to know that. People have *died* because they were unable to control their powers when playing around even with the simplest of spells."

Coura paled a little at that, averting her eyes from his. Byron cut himself off from saying more down that road as he remembered her own past. A sudden headache brought about by the conversation made him try to relax and breathe deeply. Meanwhile, Coura mumbled something to her feet and turned her gaze toward the wall on her left.

"What was that?" he asked suspiciously, hoping for some cooperation.

"I guess I didn't think about that," she said loud enough for him to make out.

"You usually don't."

Byron deeply cared about Coura for two reasons. The first being that he had found her alone and helpless to the great power inside herself. He never had children, often considering his job one that filled the need for any, but never before had he been obligated to assist and teach an orphan with nothing else but the MAA. The second, as he realized quickly into their training, was that Coura's personality was not what one expects nor encourages in a mage.

She is headstrong and defiant, always willing to jump out of line if it means proving a point. When there is something she doesn't understand, she becomes frustrated, often using power or force instead of her brain. If this behavior doesn't stop, she will not only avoid reaching her potential but need to be limited because of how strong and skilled she is. In today's case, she refused to build up her skills in favor of showing off. I know she doesn't tire as easily and the classes are beneath her abilities, but that is no excuse for acting out.

His mind cleared as he knew his point reached her, but immediately another thought came to him. A glance at the bag at his feet reminded Byron he was supposed to be heading out to Verona. He suppressed a groan at the thought of another trip, and what that meant.

Nearly every other week for the past four months he had visited the capital to meet with King Hernan and his council to discuss the possibility of a new law involving graduating students at the Magic Arts Academy. It was usually an uneventful venture, but the thought of having time to settle in to one spot tempted him more often than not. Besides, Symon had recommended him as the spokesperson on the academy's behalf, so he couldn't say no.

"Byron?"

As he turned his eyes away from the pack and back to his student, there was concern mixed with curiosity in her expression. "You look like you want to flop down on a bed and sleep for the rest of the day."

"Was it that obvious?"

"Only someone who sees you often would notice how exhausted you are. Tell me why you're always gone."

Byron chuckled and rubbed the back of his neck while Coura visibly relaxed and leaned against his desk with her arms crossed. The hint of a smile was making its way across her lips, and the difference in her tone and manners from a minute ago was like day and night. That, as he had learned over the years, meant she took his words to heart and was moving on.

"Well, I don't believe that is any of your business," he joked with a smile.

"Fine, but how much longer are you going to be doing this?" she asked, then quickly added, "Not that I miss *you*, but we both know you're the only dark mage strong enough to train me properly, and probably the only one who's willing to put up with me."

I can't argue with that, he thought about saying.

"I don't know how much more, but it shouldn't be too long," he answered instead. "Also, you can't expect to learn everything from me. It might do you some good to cooperate with your peers and instructors. As I mentioned, it will be worthwhile practice for your basic spellcasting anyway."

"Are you sure you're not saying this because your abilities are growing worse? Because if so—"

A knock at the door cut off the rest of her sarcasm before Byron could. He nearly shouted for the guest to come in, but then remembered he usually locked his office door while he packed to avoid unwanted company.

I will have to remember to lock the window next time as well.

As he strolled over to the door, Byron intentionally ended the conversation. "We'll have to continue this another time when I return, but I expect your behavior and attitude to improve. You're about ready to graduate, and I won't always be around to keep an eye on you or get you out of trouble. A master mage should be able to think about a situation and make the correct choice while following the law. Remember that, Coura."

Without hesitation, he unbolted the lock and opened the door. Byron instantly recognized his longtime friend Symon as the man slid inside with poise.

"Headmaster, to what do I owe the pleasure?" he said coolly, but not with malice, while closing the door.

"We've been through this enough to dismiss formalities, my friend," Headmaster Symon replied with a wave of his hand. He caught Coura now standing up straighter with arms at her side and with the look of someone who was expecting the hammer to fall. "I came to see you off before you left. Although, I was expecting you to be alone."

"I'm sorry," Byron apologized, then turned to Coura. "Would you mind?"

She made a motion to leave, but Symon shook his head. "Oh, there's no need. I only wanted to give you these and wish my friend a safe voyage."

He handed Byron a satchel, which, after a brief glance, Byron saw held signed documents on various matters. He usually was asked to bring anything that needed to go to the city as no one made the trek as often. Symon shot him a real smile, lifting his spirits a bit.

"I see. You just have to make sure your deeds are taken care of and the messenger boy follows through with his duty. I remember the good old days when people would ask before shoving papers at my face." Byron held his chin higher with a deathly serious expression he knew Symon couldn't stand. The headmaster tried not to laugh and failed. Seconds later, Byron joined in before noticing Coura's surprise.

She must have forgotten our history. Thinking about when we both graduated from here makes me feel old. My preference was always for offensive magic and combat, which was why I chose to join Verona's army for training. Meanwhile, Symon preferred life at his desk, working to better the future for younger generations. He is organized, honest, and as personable as necessary with a fair judgement that would make most leaders jealous.

When the MAA sought out instructors, Symon was one of the first to volunteer. It was only a few years after that the previous headmaster opted to retire and the position was open. The unanimous vote went to him, and despite his uncertainty about upholding the academy's standards, it didn't take long for Symon to adjust to the position.

"Come now, Byron, you have far more worth than a messenger boy!" Symon put on a thoughtful expression. "I would compare you more to a steed, or an ox. It suits both your build and personality."

In return, Byron rolled his eyes. "So I'm an animal now? If I am to be an ox, you must be some sort of decorative bird that spends all morning chattering."

Symon pretended to appear offended before puffing himself up and casting an eye at Coura with a frown. "Chatter I have done today indeed. You see, I seem to be hearing a rather extensive list of troubles from Coura's instructors, and, as you know, I'm obliged to inform you."

Coura's cheeks faintly blushed and she looked away from them. While Byron knew how to craft a conversation to get his message across in the easiest way possible for the listener, Symon was always straightforward with his words. In this case, Byron addressed Symon as if Coura wasn't present to help her situation.

"Yes, I've spoken with her about some of the issues she has been having, and those she is creating for others. It seems I will have to spend some extra time with her once I return because of the level she is at. Some extra work outside of classes is just what any student needs before graduating and moving on from the academy."

Symon gave Byron a questionable look. "Yes, I understand. In fact, I remember you mentioning a couple of times how much you appreciated your lessons when you left. When you were in the army, you needed them most I think..."

The headmaster gazed up in thought, leaving Byron to wonder what the man was planning. After a second more Symon nodded to himself, glanced over Coura, then smiled at Byron.

"Why, I do believe Coura is at the age to become an apprentice."

Byron shot his friend a wary look. "Yes, and?"

He better not suggest sending her away. I have had this talk with him and several other instructors more than once. I won't allow her raw potential power to be put into combat without the proper training, especially since she doesn't remember anything outside of East Hoover. Unfortunately, there is a growing chance of that happening with the contract King Hernan wants.

A few months back, Symon had received a notice from his highness that his army commanders wanted to form a contract with the academy. The new law they proposed stated that mages in the academy would train until the age of seventeen, then be sent off to the army for three years of service. After that, they could choose to stay in the palace or leave for one of the other paths available to them. The issue that brought about such wishes, according to the commander, was that fewer mages were joining the army, and, in case of war with neighboring countries, they wanted trained soldiers.

Our issue is that most mages naturally do not choose to go to the army because they either aren't built to handle the stress and sights or they lack the skills for combat. Pressure, fear, and raw emotions are dangerous for mages because they significantly impact our control over energies. That just has to be the most ridiculous concept to the king and his generals, though.

Symon's next words pulled Byron out of his thoughts before it could put him in a bad mood. This time, the headmaster intentionally spoke to Coura, who remained wide-eyed with apprehension. "Have you considered where you would like to go once you graduate?"

"Well, I thought about what I could do, but I really haven't decided on anything," she answered honestly and without any trace of the nerves she showed earlier.

"What would you say to tagging along with Byron on his visit to the capital city?" Symon said to both Byron and Coura's surprise.

Before Byron could wrap his head around the idea and dissuade his student, Coura eagerly agreed. The pair looked at him with matching grins as if the suggestion was planned. He met their looks with what he hoped was a disapproving expression while he tried to find his own stance on the invitation. However, Symon sent Coura off to pack for the journey and closed the door by the time he processed the whole conversation. The headmaster faced Byron with his chin in the air, possibly expecting a challenge.

"What prompted you to do that?" Byron asked instead. Although he trusted Symon, the headmaster was impulsive at the best of times and intolerable at the worst when it came to dealing with these types of issues.

"A few things actually. As I mentioned, I've had instructors complaining to me for weeks about her when she is not under your supervision. Normally I would shrug off a misbehaving student once they learn their lesson, or consider dismissing them from the MAA if their behavior continues. However..."

"Coura's not exactly normal."

Symon tapped his finger on his lips. "Yes, not only would there be nowhere to send her, but I must say the thought of her being alone with such potential is slightly concerning. Nonetheless, both her attitude and abilities need your hand, and yours alone. On top of that, she is of age for apprenticing. Don't think I forgot our talks either. I wouldn't let her graduate from here unless I was sure she could control herself and not tarnish our reputation."

"All right," Byron interrupted in defeat. "So there's that, but besides the obvious, why else do you want her with me?"

Symon sighed and unexpectedly appeared sympathetic toward Byron. "I *do* worry about my friend, you know. Every time you come back here, I can tell this assignment is placing more burdens on you. Also, with the risk of war upon us, at least according to what you mentioned, I want to know that you will stay safe. Even though Coura is mostly prepared to graduate, it should be a good experience for her. I'm hoping it will show her why we are so serious with training."

Byron lightened up at his words. "I like the idea; it just caught me off guard is all."

The headmaster put a reassuring hand on Byron's shoulder. "There's one other reason too."

"And what would that be?"

Symon stepped back and began opening the door. "I know without a doubt you must be so lonely! A little company could do you good. After all, I bet your morning breath wards off any living creature within a mile, and I won't even go into your cooking. I only hope the young woman can tolerate smoke and burnt meals or else she will starve to death."

"Why you…" Byron didn't have enough time to grab something to throw at him, though, since after that last remark, the headmaster slipped outside and closed the door.

So that was his way of saying goodbye, eh? Then again, that was all Byron needed from his friend.

3

"I thought our adventure would be a little more exciting," Coura said behind Byron, who turned his head to hear her from where he led a few steps ahead.

"Well, what did you expect? Remember, it takes a few days to get to the capital." He faced forward and continued at a leisurely pace.

"You don't even get a horse?" To her amazement, he only laughed and continued onward.

I guess that's a no then, she thought as she adjusted the bag on her shoulders before trotting up to walk beside her teacher. Although he would never mention it, Byron seemed to enjoy the company more than he initially let on.

Only a few hours ago the two had set out from East Hoover on their journey to the palace in the capital city. Byron was taking extra steps with her addition to make sure she behaved, something Coura couldn't blame him for doing. He even lectured her during the first part of the day on traveling safety, proper manners in a public setting, and whatever else he deemed important. She continued nodding and promised to not cause trouble, but eventually he caught on to her excitement at finally leaving the academy. That visibly eased some of his tension, and they fell into conversations about more casual topics, like local wildlife and climate conditions for the area.

That evening they settled in a clearing just off of the road. Byron assigned Coura the task of starting a fire, feeding it, and collecting enough wood to last the night, while he set up their bedrolls and cooking supplies. With no more than a wave of her hand and a touch of the energies in her center, she created sparks that caught on to the tinder. Once a basic fire was going, she rose and turned away to fetch the firewood.

"Just a moment, Coura," Byron called from nearby. When she faced him again, she was startled to see him rise and stomp out the tiny fire with one foot.

"What are you doing?"

He rummaged calmly through the bag again, pulled out two stones, and tossed them to her. She caught and stared down at them without comprehending.

"Make it again."

"Why?"

"Because I said so," Byron answered as he sat down once again and pulled out bread, fruit, and dried meats that would serve as their supper.

Coura cocked her head at him, waiting for more, and finally raised a hand once again to cast a fire spell. To spite him, she made the flame larger and it caught on to the smashed kindling. Instead of rising, Byron picked up the frying pan at his side and beat down the flames until they disappeared into the dirt while Coura watched, silent with irritation. Only after he set down the pan did he gaze up at her with some challenge in his eyes.

"Make it again," was all he said with a nod to the stones in her hands.

"I did," she responded with a crooked smile.

"Let me be more clear. Make it again, but with the fire-starting stones you're holding. Unless you think not using magic for this task is too daunting?"

They both knew this game far too well. When Byron wanted certain results, he would find a way to challenge her into understanding. However, this time she was more curious than determined to prove herself. "I will when you tell me why."

"Because I say so."

Coura narrowed her eyes at her instructor, who remained where he was. "That's not a good reason."

"Perhaps, but it is still mine to answer your question. Now hurry up, it's getting dark."

With a muttered curse, Coura knelt down next to the remains of the previous fires, arranged them into acceptable tinder, and began sliding one stone against the other until after a short time a spark flew onto what was left. She coddled the weak flame until it rose enough to not go out for a few minutes.

"There, are you happy?" She tossed the stones carelessly in front of Byron on the ground, then hurried into the edge of the campsite to grab whatever twigs and branches she could find.

"You will find more hearty pieces if you head farther in," her teacher called from that same spot. Coura ignored him and continued her task. When she collected a sufficient amount of wood, she dropped the armload into a pile before feeding her fire.

It wasn't until after they had eaten a simple supper of dried meat, toasted bread with butter and cheese, and an apple for dessert did Coura feel like making conversation. "Why did you have me use fire stones instead of magic?"

"For two reasons," Byron began as he wiped his hands on the grass. "First, we typically never use stones to make a fire. I wanted to make sure you knew how to do it just in case."

"Why would I need to, though? You taught me that mages manipulate the energy inside our center. There is energy in us as long as we are alive, right? Why wouldn't I be able to use that?"

"Well, what do you know about light and dark energies?"

Coura bit her lip. "Light energy allows some people to use light magic, and dark energy lets us use dark magic."

"That's putting it very simply, but all right. What if there is no dark energy for us to use?"

She pondered that for a moment. "When does that happen? I've never seen or heard of a mage lacking the energy to use magic."

"Try not to think of this lesson in terms of a mage not having enough energy. That will be for another time since we won't have to worry about it. What I am referring to happens rarely, but there are situations with certain circumstances when we can't use our magic, or it would be better *not* to use spells. What if you were trying to avoid detection or working with a group uncomfortable with mages? I have multiple stories where it was dangerous for me to use magic."

"Really? You never told me about that," Coura said with growing interest.

Byron nodded and went on. "In my earlier years stationed in Fester, there was a fire outside of the city. It was in an old farmhouse, and the family was terrified. I helped put out the flames while they watched. At first, I started to use a shield to keep the flames contained and eventually snuff them out. The owners of the farmhouse went mad. You see, it was magic that started that fire, so seeing me use it connected me to their suffering. Not to mention it made me a suspect in that moment."

"So, what did you do?" she interrupted, unable to imagine anyone not used to seeing a simple spell at work.

"I took down my shield and grabbed a bucket like the others. It may have taken longer and caused more damage in the end, but it brought less chaos to the already heated family." Byron gave her a sidelong glance as if expecting her next question.

"OK, I understand the first reason. What's the second?"

His lips bent into a frown. "Obedience."

"What?"

"It is no secret you have trouble following directions, Coura. I promised the headmaster and my fellow instructors I would work on that with you."

Something about the way Byron phrased his words bothered her. "Do *you* have a problem with that?"

As she expected, he paused to look past her. "I do, and before you say anything, just listen. There's an appropriate time to follow your own judgments, and also times when you should trust others and obey their direction."

"What if they are wrong? What if they don't understand the full situation?" Coura asked, reminded of her issues in class. "How can you sacrifice your own needs to blindly follow someone else, especially if you do not know them personally?"

"As I said, you should be able to understand when to follow your own instincts and when to follow someone else's instructions. In your classes, instead of using the extra time to practice or seeking help for your skills, you disrupted the other trainees' progress and got punished. Tonight, you disobeyed my orders because you didn't trust my intentions. In the army, that is seen as treachery."

"If you would have told me all of this before, I would have done it," she argued and tried to wrap her head around his words.

"You're missing the point, Coura. There is not always going to be time to explain. Sometimes you don't get an explanation because there isn't one. You have to trust your leader and their decision making. It might not turn out as you think, but no one knows for sure. Most importantly, how can you expect to earn others' trust and loyalty if you are not willing to share yours?"

"I will earn it through my own actions and decisions."

"Look where that put you with your instructors," he added with a hint of frustration. "What if your choices and actions cause harm or trouble? That may not be your intention, but there are generals you will work under in the future who have experience guiding armies toward a goal. Their soldiers risk their lives for beliefs embodied in their leaders."

"When did I mention I was going to be a soldier?" she asked bluntly.

Byron stopped at that, blinking at her as if realizing what his words implied. While she wrapped herself up in her own blanket, Coura wondered what made him assume she would join the army.

"No matter what you say, I trust myself over a stranger," she concluded matter-of-factly. "If they give me the information I need to make a decision, I can work with them, but I will never give anyone my power or skills blindly."

With that, Coura laid down, facing away from Byron as he continued to watch her. After a few moments passed, she heard him move around and then silence. His lack of a response brought a wave of guilt over her.

I do not regret what I said at all. No one should ever be forced to follow someone else's orders without knowing their intentions. Then again, I guess I see what he means about trusting in those who are more experienced and know better. Byron's voice in the quiet evening air startled her out of the self-reflection.

"Do you trust me enough to follow my orders?"

Of course, I do, she wanted to laugh at him. *I wouldn't have come along with you if I was not willing to work with you.* After a moment of thought, Coura noticed that his tone suggested more than what she heard. *That's not what he is asking. I think he wants to know if I believe in his intentions enough to follow without questioning.*

In response, she replied honestly with what she thought he wanted to hear. "Yes. I trust you, Byron."

* * *

The second day of traveling was uneventful. They passed through a small town where none of the people paid them any attention, then made camp outside of it in another clearing populated by merchants with carts or other travelers on their own business. As they settled away from everyone else, Byron explained his usual route to Coura and how, over the next three days, they would reach Verona. Each field they would camp in he had used several times over the past few months. Since the roads would only grow more populated as they neared the capital, the clearings would contain more travelers, but they would be protected and have leftover firepits to make their preparations easier.

The following morning, the duo set out once again. However, instead of taking the busier route leading through another town, Byron directed them along a rough path in the thicker part of the woods.

"Why aren't we moving with everyone else on the easier road again?" Coura asked as she pushed aside a branch covered with pine needles. There were plenty to keep her from walking casually.

"Because, this is the more scenic route," Byron answered in a carefree tone.

It was true. They saw plenty of wildlife in and through the trees that varied in color from bright and darker greens to browns and whites of tree bark with spots of floral colors. Since Coura could not remember her years outside of the academy, the sights, piney scent, and sounds of water, leaves rustling, and creatures scurrying about was new. The weather complemented the scenery as sunlight poured through the canopy above, shining on the leaves covering the branches above, around, and below them. The only downside of this path, besides its solitude, were the biting bugs, which constantly buzzed around her face. Finally, her temper got the better of her and she slapped at the bugs with no remorse.

"You sure know how to make a lot of noise in a loud forest," Byron chimed from where he hiked in front of her.

"I can't help it! I'm being bitten all over," Coura snapped back and swatted her cheek as a fly landed on it.

"Hang on just a little while longer. I remember a break in the trees coming up soon," he assured her. As promised, the trees thinned and more light poured down from above as they walked into an open field.

"Finally, I thought we'd never—"

Byron stopped Coura with an arm, freezing them both in place. She knew immediately that something was wrong by that action alone and scanned the seemingly normal space. The grassy area was surrounded by trees with a wider trail leading through to the opposite end. Near the middle, just off the path, were an assortment of wildflowers. She could barely make out a figure right in the middle of some purple flowers. They curled up on one side facing away from Byron and Coura. The arm in front of her lowered as Byron hurried toward the boy while calling out.

Coura followed without rushing and watched the edge of the trees while reaching out with her mind to sense any unknown energies. All the while she recalled stories of bandits and demonic creatures known to use innocent bodies as bait. While Byron knelt next to the boy, she stood and continued to keep an eye out around them. The forest noises chimed on, so after a moment, she relaxed and focused on the waking boy.

* * *

Byron's initial thought after seeing the young man and making sure there were no unnatural energies nearby was to check that he was unharmed. He already had mentally swept the area by instinct, and allowed Coura to do so on her own. That way, she could learn by herself what should be done in this kind of suspicious situation. However, in such a secluded area as he knew this place to be, Byron did not expect that they would need to fret over much.

"Are you all right?" he asked from where he knelt as he put a hand on the boy's forehead. After a brief inspection, Byron realized the boy was not as young as he initially had thought. His shaggy brown hair covered his face enough to barely hide a set of round glasses pressed to his cheek in a sideways position. The boy was scrawny with short, skinny limbs, but did not appear older than some of the students at the academy. There were no physical injuries, and his breathing was deep and steady.

"Is he asleep?" Coura asked with surprise from behind his shoulder.

"It seems that way," Byron muttered with some amusement before shaking the boy's shoulders slightly.

With a snort, the boy started and blinked up at them with a dazed expression. After realizing he was no longer alone, he let out a startled yelped and pushed himself away from Byron.

"I-I-I was just... Who are you? How did you f-find me? I don't have anything," he began frightfully.

"It's all right. We're not here to harm you." Byron showed his hands in reassurance. "We came here on a trail and found you laying here in the middle of the grass. Are you hurt?"

The boy blinked at them and relaxed. "I don't remember..." Byron waited patiently while he looked around and muttered to himself before exclaiming, "That's right!" He searched the ground frantically, then lifted up a purple flower with wilted petals.

"I came out here to study this!"

"What is it?" Coura asked in an unamused tone.

"It's a purple fly-lily. You see, these only bloom in areas with direct sunlight, lots of rain, and warm temperatures. I heard a rumor in Fester that they were in these woods, so I set out to find them."

Byron pushed himself to his feet and offered the boy his hand. As he accepted the gesture, Byron saw a satchel, papers, bottles, and various other utensils sprawled out around where they were standing.

"What happened to you here? Were you attacked?"

The boy flushed and looked sheepishly at Byron. "Oh no, not at all. I wanted to make sure this was the right flower, so I ground it down into an edible paste. You see, the purple fly-lily's pollen has extreme sleeping properties useful in many potions."

Coura stepped up to Byron's side and pointed at the flower. "Wait, so you thought the best way to test its pollen was to taste it for yourself? That's idiotic!"

Byron nudged his student with an elbow to stop her from scolding the boy further. She glared up at him while rubbing her side but thankfully did not say any more.

"My name is Byron, and this is Coura. We are on our way to Verona."

"I'm William Shairp, but you can just call me Will," the boy said with a friendly smile.

"It's nice to meet you, Will. As long as you are fine, I suppose we can leave you to your work," Byron said as he returned the smile.

"Actually, I'm heading to Verona as well. Would you mind some additional company for the remainder of the journey?" Will practically bobbed around like a rabbit as he gathered his things without waiting for their answer.

Meanwhile, Byron contemplated taking Will with them, but could not see any reason not to. "I suppose it couldn't hurt," he said finally and found their direction again.

"Just try not to do anything stupid," Coura commented from behind with arms crossed. If she meant any offense, Will didn't seem to notice. He only bowed slightly with some embarrassment.

"Come along, you two. We can make camp before the sun sets just as soon as we reach the edge of these woods and see the main road," Byron said as he took the lead, leaving Coura and Will to follow.

* * *

Coura knew Will's type from interacting with scholar trainees back at the MAA, and they were not her favorite people to be around. As they trekked through the forest, she grew annoyed with his constant analyzing of each tree, plant, root, berry, and item in the woods. Byron seemed more inclined to listen after sharing a little about their journey and even asked a question or two.

"Coura, you seem awfully quiet," Byron commented from the front of their line with a knowing tone. Once they were on the road, the two mages made sure to keep Will in between the reliable defenders.

"What do you want me to say?" she responded harsher than intended. Another flying bug landed on her arm, and she slapped it flat, taking small satisfaction at seeing its crushed body on her skin instead of another bite.

"You should try this for those insects," Will said quickly as he reached into the satchel at his side and dug out a bottle of some orange liquid. Byron watched curiously but didn't seem concerned.

Hesitantly, she took it from him. "What is it?"

"It's a bug repellent I made," he said proudly.

Coura opened the bottle with caution and sniffed it. To her surprise, it smelled like peppermint. "What's in it?" she asked as she poured a healthy amount onto one hand and began applying it to her arms and face.

"I'm glad you asked," Will answered as he pushed up his glasses with enthusiasm. That seemed to be the segue into the next topic of conversation as Will described in detail the various leaves used in the mixture. Afterward, he continued on with his findings for several other plants, which did not have medicinal properties on the skin and only caused rashes or pain.

Throughout the afternoon, Will told them stories of experiments that left him vomiting, dazed, numb in areas of his body, itching, and hallucinating. By the time the trio reached Byron's campsite, the sun was setting, and Coura's stomach was growling even after hearing about some of the repulsive potions or their side effects.

How can someone think to risk their safety and comfort for something like this? Coura wondered as Will went on. *I mean, it might be useful in the end, but I would never rub an unknown plant on my body, let alone eat it!*

"How's the itching?" Will asked Coura as they set down the baggage and stretched before making camp.

She raised her eyebrows and scanned her skin. The bites were no longer noticeably irritating, and the bugs had stayed off of her for the rest of their hike. Even without a verbal response, Will knew his solution had worked as he beamed at her and pushed his glasses up the bridge of his nose.

"Works great, huh? It really is the scent that gets the bugs to stay away. Like I said before, the plants in it help the itching. I put a few harmless berries in it for color, but I am planning on spreading the recipe once it's tested more. I'm still not sure how long it lasts or if it has any other properties, useful or not. There's a new plant I—"

"I'll go get the firewood," Coura interrupted at last. Her patience ran thin when he rambled, so she turned her back on the two and jogged to the end of the clearing.

* * *

As his student moved away from their camp, Byron cursed at her in his mind, even against his better half as her teacher. *How can Coura be so rude when speaking with someone so intelligent and genuine?*

Although he talked a lot, Will was honest and proud of his work, two qualities most people Byron worked with lacked. He knew some of what the boy was talking about, but as he prattled on about different types of medicinal properties, Byron found himself learning more.

Yes, he can lecture for a while, but it is all valuable information. What's more surprising is how young the boy is. I would say he is

Coura's age or close to it. I'll have to talk with her about picking up bits and pieces through these types of conversations... and also not how to offend everyone she meets.

Will watched her go, his mouth still hanging open in mid-sentence. Byron put a reassuring hand on his shoulder. "I apologize for my apprentice. She's not very good at talking to people, and she is still learning manners."

"It's all right. She's definitely not the first girl I've scared off with talk of experiments and potions, but she sure is one of the prettiest, even if she is blunt."

Byron raised an eyebrow at him, taken aback by his easygoing nature and comment about Coura. His eyes followed Will's to where she knelt down to gather some twigs a ways away.

I've never even thought of anyone finding her attractive, Byron smiled to himself as he recalled Coura's attitude toward her fellow students. Her physical features were attractive for that age, accentuated by a fit lifestyle. Even so, it was her personality that had young men turning on their heels. Memories of fights, dominating both magical and physical obstacles, and verbal bouts flooded his mind. Byron patted Will's shoulder sympathetically and started to unpack his things, letting that idea fade.

The boy brought his own supplies, which consisted of mostly foraged items, bedding, and other utensils in addition to the satchel full of research materials. When Coura returned to drop her armful of branches, Byron tossed her the fire stones.

She looked at him with annoyance as he nodded. "Really?"

Although she did not refuse this time and opt instead to use her magic, a stream of mumbled insults directed at everything filled the silence until she was able to create a spark that caught on to the kindling. All the while, Will explained some of his tools until Coura cut him off.

56

"Don't you ever shut up?" she snapped and threw the stones at Byron's feet.

"Coura," he warned with thinning patience, but Will only chuckled.

"Sorry, I tend to ramble. It's just that I am so used to being alone in the woods, and, well, it's nice to have company."

Byron expected Coura to make some sort of retort, but instead she reached for the pack for food while rolling her eyes. Together, their small group ate dinner complemented by sweet berries contributed by Will, and slept only after he thoroughly had explained different types of edible berries around this region.

* * *

The following morning, Coura felt much more energetic. The thought of reaching the capital city made her eager to be out of the woods and around buildings and people. While her companions slept, she packed up their things and practiced some spells at the edge of the campsite. As the morning wore on, she finally decided to wake Byron up to get on the road. He groggily rubbed his eyes, yawned, and got up, but it took even longer for Will to pack his things. By the time they actually started on the road, it was around noon.

"I thought we were planning on getting to Verona today," she told Byron, irritated by his sluggish pace.

"Why hurry," he shrugged from the front.

"Because I'm tired of sleeping on the ground in the woods. I'm ready for an actual bed, with warm food, servants, and a little more civilization."

"Well, I'm not sure we will stay in the palace tonight."

Coura raised an eyebrow. "All right, I guess an inn is fine. I've never actually spent the night in one, but I'm sure it's the same."

"You've never stayed at an inn?" Will asked, cocking his head in her direction. He was quieter today but would talk when spoken to or when the group went silent.

"No, I've never really needed to. I've been at the academy for most of my life."

"Oh, I travel all over the country, so I stay at inns often. Although I prefer to camp out. There's something about being away from other people that is calming."

Coura thought of a dozen different questions to ask based on his words. Instead, she let her impatience show. "Well, *I* would rather stay somewhere with a big, comfy bed," she stretched her arms in the air to emphasize her point.

"You will stay wherever I tell you to," Byron cut in, pulling out their breakfast from his pack. "Let's hurry up and eat."

Coura grabbed the bread and fruit and mumbled, "*Now* you want to hurry..."

* * *

After nearly an hour on the road with no conversation, Coura decided to learn more about their new companion. She tapped Will on the shoulder, causing him to jump and nearly fall on his face.

"So, what exactly do you do again?" she asked casually.

After recovering, he gave her a puzzled look. "What do you mean?"

"You travel to study plants and stuff, but is that your job? You don't seem that old."

He nodded, perking up at her interest. "I studied with an herbalist in Clearwater. That's where I'm originally from, the southernmost city in Asteom. When I was little, my parents had me work under him to see if I could use magic. After a few months, it became obvious that I couldn't. They wanted me to learn something else, but I really enjoyed being an herbalist anyway."

"Even without magic you can do that?"

He chuckled. "Well, yes! Herbology is the study of plants. My mentor was able to heal with his light powers, but most of our work involves putting together various species of herbs, flowers, and plants to make medicines and potions."

"I guess I never really considered what people without magic could do."

From the front, Byron growled and turned to give her an upset look. "What do you mean you never thought about it? Should I have you explain your weapons' training, or perhaps have you start a fire with only rocks?"

Coura shrugged and gazed over the woods around them. "I have magic, so I don't have to worry about those things a lot."

Whatever Byron grumbled after was lost as he turned to continue leading them down the path. When Will did not pick up the conversation, Coura left it alone. For most of the day, she watched the trees around them and became lost in her own thoughts. It wasn't until the two ahead of her stopped just outside of a busier path that anyone spoke.

"At this rate, we should reach Verona and be able to make camp before it gets dark," Byron said in a satisfied tone that made Coura sigh.

"So, if we slow our pace and *don't* have time to set up camp…"

"Then I guess the ground will be less comfortable," he responded without skipping a step. She suppressed her own groan of distaste and reluctantly followed.

The woods eventually thinned as the sun began to set, and before they knew it, the trio found themselves at the edge of an enormous field, the largest Coura had ever seen. What really caught her attention was a structure that could only be the palace, sitting in the distance with twinkling lights all around.

Byron noticed her gaping at the sight and chuckled. "Pretty neat, huh?"

"Neat does not even begin to describe it. That castle is huge! Even from this distance I can see so much."

"Yes, and now that we are here, we can make camp," he said as he dropped the bags on his shoulders to the ground. Will followed suit, plopping his things down with a huff.

As dusk turned to night and their group ate, Coura continued eyeing the structure in between bites. It appeared to stand at least four or five stories tall with lamps glowing in windows on each level, giving it a lively appearance. Shadows of tiny figures moved quickly around to make the lights blink often. The more she observed, the more curious Coura became until finally she pried her eyes away to converse with the other two.

"Why did you want to camp out here?" she asked Byron with genuine interest rather than the impatience she showed earlier.

"What do you mean?"

"We could have made it there today, if not during the night. I can tell you want to sleep here, away from the city. If you are here on business, why is it so important that we camp out instead of staying there, or at least in Verona?"

Her teacher was silent for a moment as he put away the cooking dishes with a straight face. "Well, I guess I just prefer private company."

"That's it?"

"I think you will understand better once we go inside."

"I think you're crazy for wanting to stay outdoors," Coura said with a shake of her head before turning to glare into the trees lingering behind.

For a few moments, she contemplated Byron's words. *"I guess I just prefer private company." What does that mean? We are just messengers, right? Every messenger sent to the academy has been kept away from others in their own chamber. I have never heard of any threats or assassination attempts, so why would our capital be unwelcoming?*

Across from the fire, Coura noticed Will studying her. "What?" she finally snapped sharply.

"Why don't you like the woods?" he asked with a tilt of his head, not at all bothered by her tone.

She blinked, confused by the sudden accusation. "I don't... What does that mean?"

"Ever since I joined you two, you have been scowling into the trees and talking about how much you want to leave. At least, that was my first impression."

Coura dared a glance at Byron who oddly kept his mouth shut and watched her with interest as he stretched out onto his roll. Will relaxed on his own bed and sleepily gazed up at the stars when she didn't respond.

"I guess, I don't know," she began roughly, laying with her back to the other two. "There are too many shadows and not enough room or visibility. Oh, and the bugs I can't stand."

Will only made a confirmation noise, but thankfully gave up on the subject in favor of rest. Meanwhile, Coura reflected on the question after agreeing with his observation. Blurred images of monstrous creatures from her childhood came to mind, and the memories sent a shiver down her spine.

To be honest, I never even noticed, she wanted to answer. *Now that I think about it, it's the feeling of being in the woods I can't stand, not what is in them. Maybe it's that there is not enough space.*

Yes, I bet that could be it since I am so used to fighting with weapons and magic.

Somehow the thought was not entirely convincing. No one else spoke, and eventually Coura assumed they fell asleep, but she stayed awake well into the night, contemplating those shadows and imagining them closing in on her from the empty road leading away from the lit palace.

4

The familiar sight of the palace's stone structure brought some comfort to Byron despite the stress awaiting him that day. He was the first awake with Will up and ready immediately after. When asked about his intentions once they reached the city, the boy was uncertain. Evidently, Byron could tell Will was interested in the palace but was not going to invite himself along. He saw no harm and offered instead, to the boy's relief.

For all her urgency the previous days, Coura was the last one to rise with a start. He convinced her to eat breakfast, then they packed up their things and walked straight across the long clearing until they reached the laundry space near the palace. The tired-looking servants pointed him around the nearest corner that would lead to the front gates, urging them on to continue with their own work. It was there he had the most difficulty keeping Coura and Will steady.

"Can you two please hurry," he pressed with hands on his hips in front of the two ten-foot-tall doors leading inside.

While Coura slowed her pace to gawk at the structure from various angles, Will could not seem to compose himself to his liking. Byron watched as the young man took out a tattered rag and wiped his glasses for the third time before brushing back his hair. By now it was mid-morning and they had missed the rush of workers heading in or out, but those still around gave them odd, curious glances as they hurried in either direction. Finally, he grabbed both by the arm and pulled them in close enough to have a private word.

"Listen to me," he began in a lecturing tone. "Once we are through those gates, you are my students observing me as apprentices should. I expect you to stay close by my side, do as I ask, and keep quiet. It will be important for you to listen to everyone around us as well."

"Why should we do that?" Coura asked impatiently.

"Because, while I am focused on gathering immediate information, I won't be able to pay too much attention to what is around me. Servants talk. Nobilities gossip. It is always imperative to keep your mind sharp, and your ears sharper. Think of it as a test for you to make sure you can keep up." With that, Byron lifted himself up from their huddle and proceeded through the double doors.

As many times as he had visited the palace, Byron still was in awe of the pristine entrance hall. The gates opened into a very wide space with marble flooring and an enormous staircase at the far end of the room. White pillars matching the floor, walls, and ceiling stood in two rows down the area, and statues of past kings and queens hid in alcoves along the outer walls. What made the space unique aside from its beautiful simplicity were the handful of giant stained-glass windows on the wall facing south. Each window was made with several bright colors, and when the sunlight shone through, it spread those colors on nearly every white surface. Behind him, Byron heard Will gasp and mutter to himself.

On an ordinary day like today, there were no more people than necessary passing through, and, aside from two soldiers in crimson jackets posted just inside, their trio were the only ones standing around. The hall felt very empty with only about three dozen people in it, but Byron knew when ceremonies or events were held here, it would fill to the brim with hundreds.

It seems as if everything is normal. I had been suspicious about King Hernan's council trying to meddle with our arrival, especially after how we left the discussion last time, but this trip might not turn out as badly as I had thought. Then again, once the council hears about where Symon stands on their "final proposition," I doubt we will leave on good terms. That would wait for later, Byron reminded himself. For now, he needed to let the king know about their arrival.

Without checking on Coura or Will to make sure they were still paying attention, he made his way across the hall to the staircase. The only sounds echoing around were footsteps of various people and casual murmuring. He made sure to hold himself up and appear professional in case anyone recognized who he was or where he was from. However, the lazy atmosphere helped him relax until they reached the bottom of the stairs where a page boy straightened.

Like any servant in the palace, the boy wore a plain, light brown uniform that was still a bit too big for him. Byron recognized him as he always did since the boy's master sent him every time to fetch Byron. There was familiarity in the servant's eyes, then he spoke when they stopped.

"Master Byron! A pleasure as always," he said cheerfully with a deep bow.

"It's good to see you again, Lyle. Would you be so kind as to escort us to our rooms? It has been a long few days of travel," Byron said, stretching out his back dramatically to the boy's amusement.

"Yes, sir! One moment..." With that, Lyle scampered around the staircase to a room behind and disappeared.

When he thought of Coura and Will, turning to see if they were still there, the former blurted out a question loud enough to make him cringe. "Why did you talk to him like that?"

"Like what?" he responded patiently but giving her a displeased look.

Thankfully, she caught his message and lowered her voice. "You seem so comfortable with him and knew his name."

Byron shrugged. "He's just a person, Coura. Lyle has always worked with me when I visit, so we speak casually."

"I guess I thought they were servants. It's their job to help you, so why should you need to know his name?"

He frowned and shook his head, disappointed, yet understanding of why she would think in such a way. "Like I said, servants are people too. It may be their duty to wait on us, but would you speak down to a shopkeeper or merchant? You never want to give anyone a poor impression of yourself by acting impersonal because of their life's work. Besides, it doesn't hurt anything to befriend someone, especially a servant who listens to the gossip and reports it to their master."

"I think I understand," Coura responded without a hint of humility.

The sound of light footsteps caught Byron's attention before he could say more. He turned to see Lyle scampering down the stairs above. The boy panted as he reached them but smiled up with crooked teeth and an answer.

"Master Byron, thank you for waiting. I passed along your message. The high priest Hendal requests you remain here momentarily while they make their way down to personally greet you."

As cheerful as the page boy was, Byron's heart sank, and it took years of control for him to keep his face unreadable and avoid growling in frustration. *What poor luck. Seeing King Hernan now must mean speaking with me is a top priority. If that is the case, I can assume what kind of unreasonable mood he will be in.*

"Thank you," Byron managed to say as sincerely as he could. That seemed to by Lyle's signal to leave, prompting him to bow before disappearing through a different door farther away from the stairs. Meanwhile, Will slid to Byron's side.

"What's wrong?" the boy asked with some concern.

Byron could not keep himself from frowning as he scratched the top of his head. *Will is very observant. Either that or I need to practice upholding my appearance better in these types of situations.*

"Nothing for you to worry about," he answered as Coura moved to his other side.

"Did he say the king is coming to see us?" she asked while gazing toward the top of the staircase with an unreadable expression.

"Yes." For Byron, this was yet another hoop the king's council was having him jump through. He realized then how Will and Coura might feel coming face-to-face with royalty.

Next to him, they both paled and whispered, "The actual king? He is coming here!"

"If it makes you feel better, I doubt he will pay you two any attention," Byron admitted both honestly and to ease some of their stress.

"Why is that?" Coura asked as she snapped her head to him.

"Because it is a tactic used to throw me off," Byron began, but Will interrupted with a tight voice.

"They want to meet with him under controlled circumstances. We are in their home, in a public space at a time of their choosing. Not only are they not giving Master Byron a chance to relax and think clearly, but they are giving us the impression that they have the most control over the circumstances. What those are, I don't know."

Byron blinked with surprise as he took in the words. They contained a scary amount of accuracy. "That sounds about right."

"It's almost as if you know what is going on between them," Coura poked Will in the arm with mock suspicion. He in turn brought out the cloth and wiped his glasses again, then his sweating forehead.

While they waited, Byron contemplated Symon's message, wondering if King Hernan somehow knew that things regarding the proposed law were not going to go as smoothly as he had planned.

* * *

"Where are they?" Coura groaned as she rubbed the toe of her travel boot into the polished marble floor, highly irritated with their hosts. Luckily, Byron and Will knew better than to try calming her rising temper when they did not know how much longer this would take.

Her stomach was tight with the nerves she refused to show, and she could care less about Will's explanation or the king's motives for meeting them like this. At the moment, her greatest concerns were finding a place to relax, then food. Their measly breakfast was running thin along with her patience.

I hate all of this waiting. Why does everything have to be so politically calculated? Why can't we just go to our rooms and relax first?

The silence hanging in the empty hall was interrupted by a loud laugh, muffled from behind the other set of double doors at the top of the staircase, then chattering. As she glanced around the room, Coura's body went tense at the sudden noise, and she saw servants purposefully leaving through the nearest exit.

68

A groan from Byron caught her attention before the doors opened wide to reveal a flock of men and women talking as if no one else were around.

A feminine laugh cut through the voices as a woman near the front craned her head around to speak to someone behind. "Your Highness is *too* funny!"

"Oh yes, we all enjoy your humor," a man dressed in an all-white ensemble complete with oiled-down hair threw in.

"Such a pleasant palace," a hefty, makeup-covered older woman scanned the room with a fan in her hand. "I always enjoy our visits."

Without even attempting to conceal her annoyance, Coura scowled at the dozen or so people fluttering down the stairs. Not only were their voices insufferable and echoing through the area, but their outfits were made to match. The several women clinging to one another at the front of the group wore dresses in flamboyant colors at least twice their width. Most sported hats and hairstyles as dramatic as their clothes. Coura felt her eyes widen as she noticed one woman with a stuffed bird dyed red in a yellow straw hat nesting on her head.

Honestly, this would be hysterical if it weren't so irritating, was all she could think.

The men in the group were not as outgoing with their own outfits, but each was clean with at least some piece of gold on their person. Their beards were well-trimmed and groomed to show off their features or health. Based on the characters and how they talked, Coura could only assume they were the nobility of Verona.

As the cluster of colorful characters descended the stairs, two men near the back caught her attention. Against the reds, yellows, blues, and various other color combinations, the black-and-gold outfit of the first and the cream-colored robe of the second stood out. However, their clothes were not what drew Coura's eyes. The sheer presence of the pair demanded anyone around them to pay attention.

The crown on the first man indicated his identity. The king of Asteom, King Hernan, surveyed the trio below him with un-amused eyes as he smiled thinly and followed the crowd to the bottom of the stairs. There were some who were taller than their king, but none were as broad, for the man's shoulders stretched twice as wide as Coura's. His golden hair was combed to hang along his back neatly while a similarly colored crown bejeweled with gemstones rested on his head. Surprisingly, his clothes were not that elaborate. A black vest, pants, and boots were all trimmed with gold and kept impeccably clean. Although the king's hands were clasped behind his back, she had no doubt they were calloused from years of combat training. The muscles and lean figure beneath were also proof of that, along with his poise going down the staircase.

Finally, Coura raised her eyes to his face, no doubt sculpted by years of practice in court. The square shape complemented his strong jaw and chin. There were no scars or wrinkles to mar the skin, which was slightly tanned to provide some contrast to the dark clothes. That casual smile spread across his thin lips, but even she could see he was tolerating being the center of at-tention with the nobility. Overall, King Hernan was one of the most handsome men Coura had ever laid eyes on, and she knew immediately she did not like this man.

The king's company reached the trio at last, quieting down and waiting. Hernan remained on the final step to survey the trio from above. As his deep blue eyes scanned over Byron, then Will, she realized nothing about him was genuine.

This is all just a game to these people. Until he gets whatever it is he wants from Byron, we are merely guests to be managed. Even as the thought crossed her mind, Hernan's eyes slid over to meet hers. Coura felt her heartbeat pick up and was unable to breath during those few seconds, but she held his demanding gaze. Somehow, she managed to purposely narrow her eyes a little at the arrogance behind his. She swore the smile on his lips spread ever so slightly before he returned his attention to Byron.

"Welcome once again, Master Byron of the Magic Arts Academy, to you and your students." King Hernan's voice was deep and powerful enough to make everyone in the grand hall stop to listen. Surprisingly, he sounded pleasant to Coura.

There was movement in the corner of her eye from Byron as he bowed low. She copied it in time and listened to their exchange with mixed feelings.

"The pleasure is certainly ours, Your Highness," Byron greeted the king without expression. To the flock around them, he probably sounded composed or professional. However, Coura knew what it meant when his voice was strained into a controlled, steady tone.

I wonder why he is speaking so anxiously? It's not like Byron to get nervous in front of anyone, and I thought he had been here plenty of times before. Suddenly, she remembered Will's words and understood. *It has to be because there are other people here, and not just anyone, but nobility. They like to gossip, and Byron must know that. I doubt Hernan would talk about whatever it is they are working on in public, but could he use them to influence us? I think there is more going on than I can tell.*

"As usual, you underestimate the significance of your visit," the king went on. "We are all excited to hear what news you bring from the esteemed academy. There are rumors running wild of what contributions could benefit the capital city."

Byron's face was like a statue, stiff and unmoving, aside from his mouth. "There are always plenty of ideas to make improvements or benefit certain people. As you might expect, I do bring news from the headmaster and other master mages. However, I politely request we speak in private after my students and I are able to freshen up in our room. I would hate to contribute to invalid rumors."

"I find it hard to believe a morning's travel would wear out seasoned travelers," Hernan countered with that same impassive expression.

Beneath his words, the men and women spoke in hushed voices to one another. Coura strained her ears to make out their words but struggled. She was unable to hear anything more than just their tone, which sounded confused, offended, or concerned.

Byron's expression lightened, and he even smiled in a more relaxed manner. "You would be surprised at how much young men and women complain."

Next to him, Will was blushing with his head bent forward. Coura ignored the urge to roll her eyes. *At least I know he has some humor left,* she thought bitterly.

The king's face softened as he replied. "Believe me, I know."

At His Majesty's side, the other, bald man in the simple robe leaned in to whisper something none of them could hear. Hernan nodded with a grunt and addressed the flock around them. "My honorable noblemen and ladies, I do apologize, but the representative and I have much to work out this afternoon. I offer you my deepest thanks for joining me for this morning's brunch."

The nobility caught the message, stammered their apologies and best wishes, then hurried to the front gate. Coura was grateful to watch them leave, noticing how they giggled to one another before the double doors shut with an echoing boom.

* * *

For two days, Byron met with the king and his counsel from dawn until dusk. During that time, Coura and Will were confined to one room on the second floor in the western wing of the palace under the watch of servants who brought them their meals. As soon as Coura attempted to explore on the first day, one of the older maids ushered her away.

"It'd be awfully frightening if you were to get lost in such a large castle," a first woman said while shooing her with a broom and forced smile. Within the next hour, Coura went in the other direction and was grabbed gently by the arm. A middle-aged plump woman with rosy cheeks and a no-nonsense expression told her that direction was where the servants' quarters, laundry, and one of two kitchens were. When Coura lied and said she wanted to go into the kitchen for a snack, the woman only called over a young boy, who looked scared to death at being summoned, and ordered him to bring "this honored guest" a plate of food. Obviously, the woman held some power over the servants and warned them about her sneaking about. The trip back to their room was followed by dozens of eyes.

Once she returned, Coura found Will nibbling on a platter of fruits, cheeses, and pastries brought from the kitchen with books, bottles, and herbs spread around one of the two desks in the room. She gave up for the day and went to sleep early while Will experimented in the candlelight.

The following day, Byron was still gone, and Will slept until the afternoon. Coura tried once again to survey the building but was stopped four times by servants who quickly grew tired of her escaping. The final time, she somehow made it into the grand entrance hall and walked up to the guarded gate before a page boy from the previous day popped up.

"Wait!" he shouted and gasped as if he had run to catch her.

"What?" she snapped back.

Instead of scolding her like the others, the boy smiled and bowed, showing some hesitation. "P-please, miss. You're not allowed to leave the palace grounds."

With crossed arms, Coura glared at the boy, not afraid to show her temper. "Why is that?"

She wondered what expectations the boy had for this conversation before interrupting her, for his smile dropped, his cheeks turned pink, and his eyes found the floor.

"I-I, uh... um..."

"Tell me what you know," she went on, saving him from having to make an excuse. "Why am I not allowed to leave the palace, let alone take ten steps out of my room?"

"Because that is simple palace protocol," said a cool female voice from across the room. Coura looked up to see a woman dressed in all white approach them. "That, and we council members would like to make sure no one is sticking their nose into places they shouldn't."

"I'm sorry," the page muttered from Coura's side. She was already too preoccupied with the stranger to care.

"All right, and who would you be?"

With a smile, only a slight twist of her ruby lips, the woman gave Coura a bored gaze. "I am one of the palace's personal healers and the master light mage. Normally, guests fulfill their duties and only need a room for work, meals, and rest."

Coura fumed under the woman's neutral gaze as she walked past her and the page to push open the front gate. She stopped in the doorway and spoke over her shoulder. "Servants should assist visitors while they are here, not play sitter. You would do well to remember that."

Before she could even think of a comment, the gate was closed, and the two guards seemed to inch closer together as if expecting her to go after the woman. Instead, she turned on her heel and stormed away with the page boy at a safe distance.

"Who does she think she is?" Coura growled under her breath. "What an arrogant lady with her nose so high in the air..." Insults continued to flow from her mouth, and eventually more than just the page boy behind her heard. He only continued looking at the floor, though the color drained from his face.

When she felt sufficiently relieved from the encounter, she went straight back to the room, slamming the door with one last burst of annoyance. Will was wise not to bother her for the rest of the night as she practiced punches on their pillows before easing her tension.

* * *

"This isn't fair," Coura complained and fell onto her bed dramatically. The next morning after spending a brief amount of time in the grand hall, she did not even bother attempting to leave the room save for using the washroom.

Their quarters were a simple set up containing four beds, two desks, two armoire dressers, and two windows along one wall. There was enough space for Coura to do simple exercises, even with Will working, but days without really training her body or practicing magic left her muscles twitching and energies humming. The whole while, Will studied a variety of books brought by servants and played with his herbs.

He half glanced at her with a "Hmm?" in response.

She stared up at the blank, stone ceiling in dismay. "We haven't seen Byron since we were escorted here. I wonder how he is doing."

"He's just fine," Will said flatly.

Coura sat up at his tone and saw he was carefully measuring out white powder with a tiny spoon. "How do you know?"

After pouring the substance into a bottle, he swirled it together, set it down, and faced her with a grin. "I've been staying up to read. He comes back and goes straight to bed, though he must eat with them since he is never here when we eat. Unlike you, I don't mind sitting here all day."

She impolitely snorted a laugh. "That's because you're a bookworm."

Will shrugged off her comment and went back to his work. "Although I would rather be outside, I don't have to be. It is kind of nice to not have to make my own food or keep watch at night."

"Whatever," Coura muttered as she sprang off of the bed and paced around the room. Then, she relaxed on the bed again for another minute before moving to watch over Will's shoulder.

With a huff, he took off his glasses and rubbed his eyes. "I really wish you wouldn't do that," he told her in an exhausted tone.

"Do what?"

"Pace around like a caged animal," he answered before returning to his reading.

"What else am I supposed to do?" she countered.

"I don't know, maybe ask a servant for a book to read. No one knows what you could find in a library like theirs."

Coura's head snapped to him. "You've been there?"

"Well, yes. They seem to trust me a little more than you since I know what I want and where I should be," Will said with a smirk.

"Oh, shut up," she muttered bitterly, turned away, and opened the door to the hallway. Before Coura took three steps, a servant girl her own age turned the corner with a smile and approached.

"Hello, miss, is there something I can do for you?"

"Actually, yes. Would you bring me a few books from the library?"

The girl's eyes widened slightly at the request, then she happily nodded. "Of course! I will head there straight away and be back. What sort of books are we looking for?"

Coura paused in thought for a moment. Reading was not really what she had in mind. "I'll tell you what, bring me some books you enjoy, or if you don't know, just pick whatever looks and sounds the best to you. Ask the desk worker, otherwise, I don't really care." While the girl bowed and hurried away, Coura went back into the room past Will to the first window.

"So, you are finally taking my advice," he chimed from her right.

"Not quite." With a wicked grin, she unlatched the lock on the window and pushed it open to meet a warm breeze that immediately filled the space. Carefully, Coura climbed onto the sill and swung her legs over.

Will, seeing what she was doing, rose to his feet quick enough to almost fall over. "Wait, what are you—"

"I'll be back before anyone even notices," she said with a wink from the ledge.

"Are you crazy! If you get caught sneaking around, we could get in big trouble. Not to mention what it could do to Byron's work..."

"Relax, Will. It's not as if I am going out to cause trouble. I just need to get some fresh air. If they ask, I will tell them that."

Before he could continue protesting, she flipped over onto her stomach and crawled out onto the wall.

$

Through the aching in her hands and fingers clinging to the stone, Coura was determined to reach a shadowy hiding spot as soon as possible to avoid being detected. Unfortunately, their room faced south, meaning that this early in the afternoon, most of the castle was under sunlight and would be until dusk. There were also no other buildings or trees to give her cover except for the sheets hung out by laundresses moving in and out of the palace.

A trickle of sweat tickled Coura's neck as it slid down her face and into her shirt. Her best option was to climb down the rest of the way, then sneak around to another side. Thankfully, they were near the opposite end from the laundry rooms and close to the corner turning to the back of the building. None of the busy women would notice. After descending until her ebony boots touched grass, she breathed a sigh of relief and leaned against the unnaturally cool stone to catch her breath.

It is rather dumb luck the outer wall's stones jut out enough to climb. Probably only those with the skill can pull their bodies around, but I would be cautious about leaving things like this unguarded.

The scent of fresh grass that blew up on the wind was intoxicating. For a while, Coura remained with her back pressed against the wall, cleared her mind, and enjoyed the freedom of being outdoors. It was only when the sun moved higher in the sky, heat beating down mercilessly, that she pushed off to think about her next move.

"Now what?" she asked herself and scratched her head. "I should still avoid being seen, but I'm not staying here all day."

Without knowing where exactly she was going or what she planned to do, Coura began walking. She strolled around what she figured was the back of the palace and turned the corner, only to see another stone wall extending with the one she had just passed but indented about a foot.

The brick making up this part was darker than that of the rest of the palace. It stretched for a good distance, preventing her from continuing on unless she were to move around the perimeter. The strangest part was that it acted like a fence, reaching only about ten feet tall without a roof.

"This must be a new addition," Coura concluded after some inspection. "I wonder what's on the other side."

The bricks were more even but did not make climbing impossible for her. In an uncomfortably lengthy amount of time, she managed to get herself over the top and onto the manicured grass below before ducking behind a circular bush.

Unlike the outer side that expanded out to the open field, this area was well maintained and filled with all sorts of decorative plants, trees, and sculptures. In the emerald grass grew evergreen bushes trimmed in various shapes and trees that towered well above her head, bearing ripe apples, pears, and other fruits. Amid the greenery were paths laid out in brick that matched the wall, twisting and stretching into multiple sections.

As she approached a waist-high brick wall that lined the paths, Coura leapt over after deeming the space empty. All of her thoughts focused in on the beauty that was this garden, for that was the only word she could think to describe it. What she dismissed as random paths actually intertwined with one another and branched out into different sections with unknown purposes.

The first path she chose went far back, away from the castle. In fact, Coura was worried she would find herself leaving the grounds without even realizing it. However, it curved suddenly to the right and opened to a small pool decorated with pink and purple plants. A flowering cherry tree with white blossoms swayed in the gentle wind, and its perfumey scent was divine. There were no towels, brushes, or soap around, so she assumed it was a relaxing area meant for cooling off in secrecy. It was difficult in the summer heat, but Coura suppressed the urge to splash water on her face and wash away the accumulating sweat.

Turning away from the pool, she cut across an open area of grass spotted with rose bushes to another that led even farther from the palace. This was the only path that went this far, as she soon realized. All of a sudden, there were faint voices. Quieting her steps, Coura continued forward until she could hear them better. There was a woman's laugh, and then another voice, a man's. It was impossible to understand their conversation, and she decided she would rather get caught wandering than eavesdropping on potentially important people.

After backtracking her steps, she wandered down a path closer to the palace. Here, the area opened to a more decorated floral bed with carved wooden benches, and she found this place to be absolutely relaxing. Almost relaxing enough to forget she was trespassing. As Coura shrugged off the thought, a glimmer in the distance caught her eye. Without thinking, she moved toward the source with curiosity.

In another space surrounded by bushes for some privacy stood a fountain with a statue of an angel. There were more benches here, so she picked a seat in frontal view of the piece, taking in the magnificent image before her.

The angel—seemingly made of pure white marble, to her surprise—stood nearly seven feet tall. In his right arm was a sword that appeared sharp enough to be the real thing, poised in a victory pose with the blade horizontally above his head. In his left arm, the angel held a vase with intricate markings in gold, laced perfectly. Water flowed from its tipped opening, as if the angel controlled how it was poured. He wore armor, nothing Coura was familiar with, but it was the wings behind him that held her gaze. Instead of being blocky or hard like a normal statue, the wings appeared real. Each feather was crafted with such carefully smooth lines and meticulous detail. Everywhere her eyes fell on them was different; no two feathers were the same.

The level of artistry is indescribable, she thought in awe.

Behind the wings stood a structure built like a tree in the shape of a "T," and more water trickled down from the top bar to create a thin waterfall effect. There were no imperfections Coura could find. In fact, the harder she looked, the more intricacies she found.

Although the fountain as a whole was marvelous, Coura could not help but continue staring at the lifelike wings. For a long while, she fantasized about what it would be like to see an angel and feel its pair. Would they be heavy, like an extra set of arms, or as light as many feathers? How much work does it take to carry a person her size? Are they as soft as real feathers, perhaps a chick's? What if she had a pair of her own? The last thought struck a nerve.

Where would I go? I can't even figure out where I am going to go and what I should be doing. I can't stay with Byron or at the academy forever, but I'm ... just not sure... Her eyes dropped to the grass at her feet. For a while, she sat like that, content to be alone with her thoughts.

"Beautiful, isn't it?" a male voice said from behind.

Although she was startled, Coura managed to turn casually to glance at the man interrupting her peace. Before she could voice her annoyance at being disturbed, she paused.

The stranger, a young man near her age, dressed similar to the noblemen from their first day at the palace, though less abstract. His loose shirt of crimson was trimmed with gold that gleamed in the sunlight and reminded Coura of the fountain's vase. Golden hair trailed down to his neck, and on his head rested a gold band.

A crown, Coura realized with no small amount of shock. *I'm trespassing in a private area after sneaking outside, and of all people, I run into a prince!*

Quickly, she took in the rest of his features that only confirmed his lineage: the lightly tan skin, deep blue eyes, and square face. After racking her brain for what little knowledge she possessed of the royal family, she remembered only one child of the king and queen, their only heir.

Despite his similar appearance to Hernan, there was something that separated the young man in front of her from the arrogant, haughty king. Across the clean face stretched a smile so unlike his father's, Coura thought he might be adopted. Again, though, the rest of his features suggested otherwise, especially those eyes. They were identical in shape and color, but where the king's were cold and calculating, the prince's seemed to be full of life, taking in as much as they could.

That was when Coura could feel the awkward tension. The prince picked up on it too. "You've been staring," he said, his voice informal.

She couldn't help herself from blushing before making a silly retort. "I believe you were the one who interrupted me."

What a fool I am, a complete idiot! Looks can deceive, and if he shares this brief encounter with his father, there is no telling the consequences.

The prince was visibly taken aback at such brash words, so Coura turned back to the fountain to hide her face and wait for the sword to fall.

To her utter surprise, he chuckled. "Forgive me, lady, it's not too often I am able to speak first. Most folks usually lead the conversation before I can greet them properly."

"I'm not a lady," Coura said quickly over her shoulder and caught his eye. He seemed to already know.

"Any beautiful woman deserves to be treated like a lady," he said with that charming smile. Coura turned away again to conceal another blush.

"You're right. About the statue, I mean," she said, changing the subject.

"Ah, yes. It's one of my father's favorites. A gift from the Yeluthians at his wedding. Not that they actually came to the ceremony, but he and my mother never complained."

"I don't think I have ever seen such work. It's so lifelike. The sculptor is truly blessed with talent," she admitted honestly.

"They say the angels of Yeluthia have materials and special tools to manipulate their art, making it more realistic. This is the only piece I know of belonging to a human."

Coura could think of no other comment, so they watched the fountain's waters flow in silence, it's trickling the only sound in the garden for a few minutes until he cleared his throat.

"I'm Prince Aaron. I never properly introduced myself."

"I know who you are," she partially lied without making eye contact.

"Why do you speak to me so informally then?" he countered with something sharp in his voice.

There it is. I've overstepped my boundaries. However, even with his title hanging over her, Coura dared more conversation. With a shrug that suppressed her nerves, she chanced a look up at the prince with a weak smile.

"I enjoy speaking with most people when they do not have a hidden motive for talking to me. At least, I hope you don't have one."

He returned her smile with an amused one of his own and clasped his hands behind his back. "I see. Well, I must be going." Coura watched as the prince began walking toward the palace.

"Oh," he paused and looked over his shoulder to meet her eyes, "I suggest you let the guards know when you would like to visit the queen's personal gardens. We'd hate to have any accidents in such a lovely place."

* * *

Coura's body trembled from her encounter with the heir for minutes after he disappeared. She was stunned by his generous warning, or threat. *The queen's gardens? I've never heard of such a place. There were no guards, nothing to prevent me from sneaking in here. Then again, how many people climb over a wall like that from the outside? I better get on before anyone else finds me.*

She rose immediately and made her way to the wall closest to the fountain and followed it away from the palace until she found a spot mostly hidden by fruit trees. After climbing over unseen, she strolled away, pretending to have nothing to do with the place while her mind raced.

How long have I been away? I doubt Will was able to hide the fact that I left, especially to Byron. Coura stopped and glanced up at the sun in an effort to gauge the time. During her exit from the garden, she didn't climb over the same wall used to enter. Instead, she fled from the other end, leaving her now on the opposite side of the castle as their room.

It looks like I will have to go around again. Unless I can manage to sneak inside, but I would probably get caught. Not to mention how the servants and their masters will all react. I would be locked inside with guards at the door. No, if I am to be caught anyway, I think I can explore a little more before my imprisonment.

She made it to the next corner of the building, which was not far considering the vast size of the queen's gardens, and continued. This side was similar to its opposite in that it was simply a field with woods looming farther beyond. However, near the front of the palace were several stables and huts with figures moving about. Some were walking around in the open space, but most seemed to be gathered near the largest structure. It took Coura a moment to realize that around the edges of the area where the grass met the trees was a stone wall that appeared to be three or four feet tall.

As she continued on, keeping close to the palace's wall, there were echoes of whacking noises and chatter from the group nearby. That was when she could make out their movements and the weapons in their hands.

This must be their soldiers' training grounds, she realized with genuine interest and paused. There were no doors that she could see, aside from one with people coming and going. *If I get close, they are sure to notice. I don't think they would let a stranger roam in from out of nowhere. So, what can I do?*

After weighing her chances of sneaking by or going back around to the other side before dark, Coura straightened and suppressed a grin. *Byron is going to kill me. I'm going to be in trouble regardless of which route I choose, so I should satisfy my curiosity before his punishment.*

Instead of moving toward the door leading inside the palace, she went straight to the group nearest to the stable. There were about thirty men and several women all practicing sword work with wooden practice blades and a partner. Coura recognized the moves from a distance as basic defensive maneuvers and wondered how educated they were.

Curiously, she flowed around each pair, observing their work. Most did not care and focused on their own partners, but some stared at her with either arrogance or annoyance. She ignored their looks, concentrating more on the exercises and comparing them to what she knew.

Like I would let any of these soldiers intimidate me, she thought as she noticed many flaws and uncertainty with their skills.

"What are you staring at?" a man who appeared to be only a few years older snapped at her suddenly. She had been watching him at the moment his partner successfully parried a blow accidentally.

"Your swords," she admitted without taking her eyes off of his practice blade. At the academy, her original weapons master started them out with wooden swords too until they were competent enough to work with actual, deadly ones.

"Yeah, well, this isn't the place for strangers, especially little girls," the brute sneered and turned back to his partner.

Coura thought about letting it go but could not stop the words from coming out after his comment. "That probably is for the better. I wouldn't want anyone to see me either if I were bold enough to pretend I was skilled at this."

Those around who heard halted with interest. It was not directed at her, she saw, but at the man she insulted, to see his reaction. He did not disappoint.

With a growl, the man spun to face her. Coura lifted her eyes, face neutral, and met his glare. "Who are you?" he said through clenched teeth.

She wondered what would happen if she told the truth and revealed that she was a student from the Magic Arts Academy. Would they think of her as an ally, a threat, or not worth tolerating? In the end, she shrugged and kept it to herself.

"I just know a thing or two about sword work."

He raised an eyebrow and glanced to those around him who also showed a mix of doubt and surprise. To her own amazement, he backed down and grumbled, "Whatever," at her before facing his partner again. That seemed to be the others' cue to return to their own work and ignore the stranger.

Despite her luck, Coura felt more offended than relieved that no one paid her any attention. "You are a lot less aggressive than I gave you credit for. It's no wonder you're no good at fighting with a sword," she teased with arms crossed.

Any self-restraint he had vanished as he spun around furiously. "I was trying to be nice because you're a woman, but I see you must not be worth wasting manners on!"

Without hesitation, Coura approached his partner as the man was yelling. "May I?" she asked, extending a hand toward his wooden sword.

The boy, for he was no older than Coura, whispered, "Are you sure?" She ignored him, and he eventually gave in.

All eyes fell on the stranger taking on an older male. She reveled in it, savoring the attention as she weighed the wood in her hands and spoke.

"I've seen children pick up weapons and learn to use them without having the heart to match the progress. Skills take time and effort to develop, but if you are not able to put your emotions, your *being* into them... Well, let's just say it is not going to work out for you." Coura raised her sword and pointed it at the man, who watched her with intensity. Then, without warning, she charged, intending to swipe right.

He was caught off guard but responded well enough to raise his sword. The crack that resulted echoed around the training ground, followed by silence. The man stood gaping at the sword, which was nearly split in two along the blade.

"How did you... It's broken!"

As casually as she had taken the practice sword, she handed it back to its owner, who watched her with wide eyes. Not full of fright, though. In fact, as she leveled a glance at each trainee, Coura saw only curiosity and awe, but no fear. That surprised her more than she was willing to admit.

For their lack of skills, these soldiers sure are made of tougher stuff.

"Remember what I said before?" she responded calmly. "When you fight with a sword, you have to fight with intention. I charged you with the full intent to break your arm." The man's eyes widened, and there were murmurs from behind.

Coura turned to see those around parting for another man. He was very plainly dressed in all brown, which matched his shortly clipped hazel hair and eyes. Unlike her opponent, this man appeared to be around her age.

"What is going on here?" he asked with some authority.

She kept silent while the boy she borrowed the sword from blurted out an answer before anyone else. "Marcus, it was incredible! This girl showed up and took my sword and then struck a blow at Remy that split his sword. We all saw it!"

Around the group the soldiers nodded eagerly, even Remy. All the while the newcomer watched Coura with narrowed eyes, sizing her up. Against her urge to do or say something, she remained silent with a bored expression.

He smiled at the younger boy. "Thank you, Jorge. Would you get me two blades from the armor station?"

While "Jorge" scuttled off toward the largest building, Coura stood with the stranger as the group surrounding them murmured to one another. Finally, she decided to break the tension.

"So, I take it you are in charge of their training?" The man, Marcus, didn't reply, which irritated her. "Usually you introduce yourself when you burst into the center of a group."

"All right, go ahead," he countered her with a sly smile.

The boy returned then with two polished *real* swords whose blades shone in the sunlight. Marcus took one and weighed it in his hands. "Very good. Now, give the other to..."

"Coura," she supplied and grabbed her own without taking her eyes off of her next opponent.

I will be glad to knock that smirk off his face, she thought bitterly and took her stance. Marcus mirrored her movement fluently. *So, he knows how to fight. I can tell right away he will be more of a challenge.*

Coura chose to take the offensive, but before she could move, her opponent charged, sword raised. He grunted and brought it down diagonally to hit her neck. She blocked the blow with ease and pushed his blade away with some effort. He followed with three more swings at her sides. She ducked around the first two

90

and knocked the third away with her own sword before counter-
ing with a strike to his thigh that was deflected.

*That last attack had strength behind it, which means he either
thinks I am causing trouble and wants to teach me a lesson, or he
believes I actually know what I am doing. Either way, he's too strong
to take head-on. I will have to use a lighter technique.*

* * *

"There are three main categories of weapons work I've seen over
the years," Coura's beginning teacher explained. "First, and the
most common, is strength-based. When you are on the offensive,
you put a good majority of your muscle behind attacks. For some
people who are stronger and physically larger, this is the best
way to knock your opponent off their balance. It is also intimi-
dating for fighters without too much experience. The blows are
direct. You cannot hold anything back. This category is for blunt
weapons and swords.

"The next is the swift-based, for those of you who make up
for a lack of strength with speed and agility. Usually fighters
good with daggers, knives, or other small weapons find this to
be the best for them. Lastly, there's the distance-based fighters.
If you don't like close combat, this one's for you. Most of the time
you have a preference for strength or agility, but this category
focuses on avoiding all of that with precision. Of course, you will
have to be trained in close combat too, but this adds an extra
means of fighting with throwing knives, a bow and arrows, and
even javelins.

"Now, there are two rules to follow with weapons work. The
first is that you're all fit to wield a certain weapon or two based
not only on your physicality but also by your own preference.
I've seen sprouts think they are tough enough to stab a man with

a sword who did not have the heart to put their weight behind blows. Likewise, there have been brutish students who exploded when their throwing knives couldn't hit a target because they expect them to obey, like they have that control. You *must* find the balance you are comfortable with and go from there. That's why your later years here will focus on what you can and want to work with.

"The second rule is why we train you in them all right away. Each weapon can be used in multiple ways, but you'll never be well-rounded unless you're flexible. If you lack strength, there's no reason for you to fight with a mace, and if you're too muscular, don't you dare think you can dance around with a dagger only. You will have your specialty, but what if you lose your weapon or don't have access to one? Then what will you do? A competent fighter can pick up anything and figure out how to use it to his or her advantage. This requires finding your strengths and weaknesses, then adapting." After that, he had them all choose the weapon they felt best suited for. Coura never hesitated when she picked up the sword first.

* * *

Coura and Marcus traded blows, meeting each other with precision. They huffed in the afternoon sun, and both bodies began gleaming with sweat. Never once did Coura take her eyes off of him or think of how much time had passed. Marcus struck at her right side while she rolled into his sword, sweeping under the blade and parrying with a similar blow. He was too slow. Her sword scratched his left hip. The cut was not deep but enough to distract. A hand went to that side and his sword lowered. Marcus was now breathing deeply. Coura licked her lips in anticipation.

This is it. He let his guard down. She charged, planning to strike his right arm hard enough to have him drop his sword and for her to claim victory. As her sword rose, she met his eyes and saw the corner of his mouth turn up. *Something's not right*, she realized frantically. However, it was too late.

Her sword began to fall as his rose to meet it. At the same time, Marcus sprung straight up and launched himself at her. His left shoulder slammed into her chest, knocking the breath out of her, while the flat of his sword smacked her right elbow. Coura released her weapon and fell backward.

* * *

The stranger's sword's metallic clang on the ground was the only sound for what felt like minutes. No one around Marcus seemed to be breathing.

I'm sure they are loving this, he thought as he relaxed a bit to wipe the sweat off his brow. *They've never actually seen any serious fighting from me before now.*

He kicked the young woman's sword behind him and out of reach, waiting for her to rise. After a few seconds, she still did not move. His comrades murmured around him, and Marcus's stomach twisted.

I thought I pulled that attack. I had no intention of harming her or laying her out. What did I do?

With growing panic at the consequences of hurting an innocent person, he walked over to where she lay on her back with her limbs spread out. Marcus noticed immediately the welt on her elbow beginning to swell. He hesitated to kneel beside her, not wanting to startle her awake.

"Should I get a healer?" someone in the crowd asked him. Their presence made him decide to take the professional route and not leave her in the dirt.

"Yes," he began, kneeling beside her. "Tell them it is not urgent, but—"

Without warning, the young woman's right arm shot to his side and struck him on the spot where she had scratched him earlier. It was not a serious wound, but was deep enough that the blow had him clutching his side. That was when one of her legs kicked him in the back of the head, sending him face-first into the dirt, seeing stars. When Marcus pushed himself into a sitting position, the woman was standing over him with his sword in her hand and the tip at his chest.

He was stunned, as were those around them, until their audience began shouting insults.

"Disgraceful!"

"Where's your honor in a fair fight?"

"That's not how you duel!"

"How could you fake an injury like that?"

To her credit, she ignored the jeers and continued to keep her focus, and his sword, on him. Marcus sighed and raised his hands in defeat, careful not to let his annoyance show too much.

"I give," he said, pushing the blade away as he rose to his feet and brushed off the dirt now covering him. She eyed the others around them. Most were still fuming, but the voices faded away when he was on his feet again.

"Cheater," someone muttered under their breath loud enough for him to hear, and the rest nodded in agreement.

She shrugged indifferently. "It's not cheating. A fight is a fight. You go until one person forfeits, is *actually* knocked out, or dies." The last words hung in the air, and Marcus hoped his comrades would take them to heart after his experience.

He cleared his throat to draw their attention, intent on breaking their group apart before questioning the stranger. "Now then," he began. However, a booming voice cut him off and startled most of them.

"There you are!"

A middle-aged man looking very tired and upset shoved his way to the middle of the circle, glaring at the girl. She was obviously taken aback as well but dropped Marcus' sword and moved to meet him.

"Byron, I—"

"Come, now," he ordered. Reluctantly, she moved to his side. He tightly gripped her arm and pulled her into the palace.

Marcus remained where he was, not wanting to interfere, and ordered the group to pair up again to practice their basic sword work. The rest of the afternoon he fielded various questions about that fight, not sure himself if being chivalrous had been the right thing to do with the stranger.

6

"Ouch, stop! You're going to bruise me," Coura whined under Byron's grasp. Only when they were well into the building did he release her, but he continued forward without comment. If he stopped for long enough, he knew his temper would snap.

I am already on a short stretch, and Coura likes to toy with it.

"Hey," she called from behind him. Byron ignored her until they reached their room. Will was right where Byron had left him: at his desk with his nose in a book and potion materials spread all over. When he returned earlier to find Coura gone, they had a mutual understanding that when he brought her back, things would get heated.

Once in the room, Byron went straight to the tray of finger foods brought in by a servant earlier and took a handful of options. Coura closed the door behind her and stood patiently with arms crossed. Thankfully, she had been lectured enough to know he would be more reasonable after he cooled off and ate something. After scarfing down the snacks, he opened up the wine left with the tray and took a couple of swigs. When he felt mentally prepared to deal with her accustomed lack of cooperation, Byron began.

"Why were you outside of the room?"

"Are you really that upset?" she asked back, laying on her bed and spreading out.

"Why were you outside of the room?"

She refused to meet his leveled stare. "I'm not like Will. I can't stay cooped up here all day and night."

"You were supposed to stay here," he snapped back, letting his temper show. However, with Coura, showing your own anger only brought out hers.

She sat upright in the bed and threw her hands in the air. "I can't believe you are making such a big deal about it! What is so wrong with wanting some fresh air?"

"I asked the housekeepers to make sure you both stayed here for your own safety and for the sake of my mission."

Coura's eyes widened. "You ... ordered them to keep us here? How could you do that? Don't you think we are capable of handling ourselves?"

Byron let her vent for a moment before releasing a sigh. "I thought you were smarter than that, Coura."

The disappointment in his voice was evident. It stopped his student, and she finally seemed to *see* him. "Byron, you look like you haven't slept since we got here."

"I haven't. The hours I am able to come back here to rest are few. This law could have a major impact on the academy, and negatively if it's not taken care of properly. King Hernan and his council do not see our side, so I spent all day arguing. I'd rather not spend my *whole* day arguing, if you mind," he said pointedly to her.

She sighed and glanced out the window with less attitude. "You know I have never been good at following directions."

"Do you really not understand why I did this?"

Coura paused in thought. "You wanted us to stay safe in case anyone attacked us, maybe to use as a tool to get you to do what they want."

"Not only that, but because your interactions could impact their emotions or impressions of the academy."

She looked away as her cheeks grew rosy, making Byron's stomach sink. *She has gone and done something stupid, that much I can tell. In any case, I do not want to know right now. I'm barely able to stay awake.*

The room fell silent. Byron followed her gaze out the window. Will continued working as if they were not there.

"We have a few hours until we've been requested to join for a private dinner. I plan on resting up, and I think you should go ask a servant for something for your elbow," Byron said to Coura after kicking off his boots. It took less than a minute for him to fall asleep when his head touched the pillow.

* * *

A formal dinner with the royals and nobility was cause for the three of them to wash up and dress their best. When Byron agreed to take Coura along with him over a week ago, he insisted she bring one "presentable" outfit for such an occasion. She brushed down the wrinkles on her favorite emerald dress, then began braiding her hair. Most students did not feel the need to bring their own formal clothing, or some like Coura did not have any, so the MAA kept a wardrobe full of dress clothing for students to borrow. Only twice had Coura ever needed a dress, and she chose this one each time.

"Are you two almost ready?" Byron stood with arms crossed in the doorway. He wore a deep blue shirt with brown pants and newly polished boots, courtesy of the servants. His hair was combed neatly, and his nap helped remove some of the strain on his face.

"Coming," Will squeaked from the other side of the room. He hopped on one leg as he put on a black boot. Coura finished her braid and watched as Will finished patting himself down.

Since Will had been traveling, he had no extra room for formalwear. One word from Byron and a servant boy returned with what he deemed "acceptable" dinner clothes, consisting of black pants and boots, a white long-sleeved shirt, and a deep green vest. The whole outfit was a few sizes too big, but hopefully no one would notice or feel the need to comment.

"Let's get going," Byron said as he turned down the hallway. Coura followed, while Will trailed behind.

"This is exciting," he chimed from the back, nerves making his voice unnaturally high.

Coura rolled her eyes. "Why? Byron's been eating with them for days."

"Actually," her teacher interjected, "the meals we shared in between and during most meetings were not very extravagant. Delicious, yes, but hardly what we will be experiencing."

That only added to Will's anticipation. "Wow, so is this like in the songs and stories? I heard many about how only the finest musicians play for the royal family, and sometimes they have performers there to entertain guests. Do you think they will have something like that here, Master Byron?"

"I don't know, Will, but I doubt it will be anything but relaxing for us."

"Why is that?" Coura asked suspiciously.

"Let's just say our council group grew heated, and not everyone agreed with the final decision."

"Oh yeah? What would that be?"

Byron shot her a warning look over his shoulder, which she expected.

As they approached a door near the center of their floor, he faced them with a stern expression. "Listen to me, I do not want you to speak unless spoken to. Keep your heads down and ears open. Most likely you will be ignored again. Will, keep yourself in order, and Coura..." Byron paused, then rubbed his eyes. "*Please* behave." Before she could retort, he pulled open the door to the dining hall.

Compared to every other part of the building, the dining hall was what Coura thought of as a "palace." She was momentarily blinded by the amount of light compared to the dimly lit halls. The marble floor shone under the many candles from around the room, including those hanging on a crystal chandelier in the middle of the ceiling. Two sturdy wooden tables and benches lined the length of the outer walls of the room. A slightly smaller table connected to one end of each long table, forming three sides of a rectangle. It was obvious who the head table was for, as it stood a foot taller than the other two.

However, it was not the setup of the room nor its many lively inhabitants that caught Coura's breath but the artistry. Walls and ceiling were a warm cream color with beautiful, lifelike paintings in bright, lighter colors. Scenes of nature, dancing, laughter, and more seamlessly weaved into one another.

Coura composed herself quickly and followed Byron to their seats to the right of the head table, vowing to spend the evening enjoying the art. Similar to their "welcome," the lords and ladies were strutting around in their finest dresses and robes like showy birds. As Byron predicted, the trio was ignored for most of the evening. King Hernan didn't so much as look in their direction, which was fine by Coura, though she did notice the eyes of his bald adviser, who she learned was the high priest, several times.

The dinner was phenomenal. Trays with fresh fruit and pastries were brought around by servants first, then vegetables cooked in a sweet sauce, roasted potatoes with herbs, and the juiciest venison roast Coura had ever tasted. More wine was served just before dessert, and although she was stuffed, Coura continued to marvel at the artwork decorating the room.

"It really is something, isn't it?"

She turned to see Byron watching her with a faint smile and nodded at the first words any of them had spoken since they entered the room. "It was the first thing I enjoyed about this place," he went on calmly. "Queen Freya may be shy, but she supports art and music fervently. From what I know, she *made* the king do all of this. He even let her turn the back of the palace into her own personal garden space. Maybe you will get to see it one day."

Coura glanced at her empty plate to cover her blush. "Yeah, maybe."

Finally, the dessert course, consisting of berry tarts, jams on crackers, and more pastries, was served. Content and full, she sipped on the last of her sweet wine, surveying the room casually.

Several musicians performed at the end of the meal. All played some sort of instrument and about half sang as well. At the moment, a young man was performing a soft ballad on a small guitar. A good portion of the dozens of guests had left before now, and those remaining conversed with one another in low voices. Coura was about to ask Byron when they would make their leave when a glance at the head table put her in eye contact with a familiar face.

Prince Aaron rose from next to his father with grace and made his way to where they were seated. Every step made Coura nervous until he was in front of Byron. *I hope he doesn't mention our meeting...*

"Master Byron, we are very honored you were able to stay one more night to dine with us," he said in a friendly manner.

"As you know, it's been a long week. I could not imagine leaving without a proper night's rest, and without making sure I eat enough of the wonderful food!" Byron responded.

Perhaps it was Coura's imagination, but the prince seemed to relax a bit as he chuckled. "You and your guests are always welcome here. Speaking of guests," he turned to Coura, "I am pleased you admire the artwork, Lady...?"

"Coura," she supplied quickly without expression. Aaron winked in response and continued chatting with Byron. From her right, Will watched the musicians across the room.

"Don't you hate how they ignore us," she leaned over and whispered.

"Not really," he answered without removing his eyes from the entertainment. "They all seem to belong here. We are just Byron's company after all, so it's not really their concern to talk to us."

Coura sighed and watched the musicians as well. "I know that. I hate being left out is all. These people think they are so much better than us too. If I wanted to, I could..."

"You could what?" Will turned to her with a wary expression.

"Nothing, I'm tired is all," she said finally and turned her attention elsewhere.

I could hurt them. Easily. That was what I thought, and it's true too. There would be no one to stick their nose up at us. Coura dismissed the concept entirely, but only after considering the idea, and that concerned her.

The next morning, Byron had Coura and Will up at dawn to begin their return to the academy. Against protests from Coura and groans from Will, Byron made them eat cold sandwiches for breakfast as they waited outside the front gate instead of a hot meal that could be brought to their room. They ate in silence and waited for their final companion. Byron made sure to mentally prepare himself before letting the other two know they would be joined by a guard. As he finished his own food, Coura opened another wrapped sandwich and dug in with vigor.

"I tell you," she said around a mouthful, "this place may be unbearable, but at least their food is good."

"There is one other thing before we leave," Byron caught their attention by saying.

"What is it?" Will asked while wiping off his glasses.

"We are going to have one other person joining us on our way back to East Hoover."

"What? Why?" they both asked, Will with worry and Coura with irritation.

In a quieter voice, he explained the reason. In case anything were to happen to him, or more importantly, the documents he carried in his bags regarding the proposal, the guard would either alert the king of the issue or take them to the academy himself.

Unfortunately, that is not the main reason. They do not trust me to follow through with my end of this, Byron thought with dread. He didn't dare tell Coura or Will. The former would overreact, and the latter wouldn't understand. Instead, he reassured them it was for extra protection because the documents were so important. It was a half-truth, but it worked. The two relaxed a little and finished their meal.

"Where is he?" Coura asked mid-stretch. Out of the corner of his eye, Byron noticed movement to their right.

From the other side of the palace, a young man made his way to them. He wore no armor, only a simple outfit, a pack, and a sword at his waist. Byron sensed no magical energies, which matched his ordinary "brown hair, brown eyes" profile. Upon approaching, he held out his hand, and Byron shook it briefly.

"Assistant General Marcus Tont, reporting as your guard for our venture to the Magic Arts Academy." The boy, probably a year or two older than Coura, saluted Byron.

Behind him, Coura let out a "humph," and Marcus turned to see her leaving toward the woods.

"I guess we'd best be on our way," Byron said, confused. He turned to see Marcus grinning and led them to follow Coura.

* * *

The group was surprisingly quiet as they walked down the road, so Byron decided to ease some of the unspoken tension. "Well, General, you seem to have accomplished a very honorable title in a short amount of time. I hear to earn such a place in the army is no easy feat."

Marcus, who kept eyes and ears visibly alert, turned his head to him with a friendly smile. "Please, call me Marcus. I'm actually considered an 'assistant' general. I don't want to lie about such an important title."

"Assistant general?" Byron raised an eyebrow in curiosity when the young man nodded.

"Yes, sir. How familiar are you with military ranking?"

"I know the basics..."

"Not a thing," Will said from in front of them. The boy slowed his pace to walk on Marcus's other side. "I'm very interested, though. Can you start with the basics?"

At first, Marcus showed some surprise, but then he shrugged. "Well, the easiest way to think of it is like a pyramid. At the bottom are the new members and general third class, foot soldiers and rookies in training. They make up the majority of the army. The second class are assistant generals like myself, cavalry soldiers, or those who have their own horse or go buy one to fight on, and appointed section leaders."

"The top class must be the generals," Will interrupted.

"Right. You will also hear them called captains or commanders. It's the same title for the highest ranking."

"How many generals are there?"

"Four."

"Only four? I thought there were hundreds of soldiers…"

"There are, but most of the disciplining and delegating goes to the section leaders. Each soldier is categorized into a single division with a supervisor."

"So, then you're in charge of your own division?"

Marcus shook his head. "I'm an assistant general. My duties are to work directly under the generals and pass along information. We are sort of like the middlemen between the first and second classes. At the same time, we learn from our supervising general so that we may move up in our ranking."

Byron could sense there was more Marcus was not telling them. "How do you move up in rank?" he pushed when the soldier went silent.

"I wish I knew."

"You mean you don't know?"

Again, Marcus shook his head. "It is up to the judgement of my supervising general. When they deem you worthy, you'll be appointed to your new position."

"That sounds awful," Will said in disbelief.

"They do not mention when you're close or if you are doing anything right or wrong," Marcus said, more to himself than to them.

"Think of it this way," Byron told Will in a lighter tone. "In the academy, it is up to the discretion of the instructors when a student graduates and what they will do afterward. That's because we work with students long enough to understand when they are ready to move on. If the army is anything like the MAA, their leaders will use honest judgement based on actions and attitude. As long as my students are hard-working, honest, and good-hearted, I know they will succeed and trust in my decisions."

The answer satisfied both Will and Marcus; however, Byron kept a close eye on Coura up ahead. When he began to talk with them, he sensed her ears perk up in curiosity.

I can only pray she takes my words to heart.

* * *

The first evening, no one argued when Marcus offered to keep watch during the first half of the night and Byron the second. They made camp in another similar resting area often used by travelers, as the recently banked firepit showed. It did not take long after dinner for Coura to hear Byron's light snoring and Will's heavy breathing.

As she tossed and turned, she caught a glimpse of Marcus perched against a log with a candle in one hand and a thin book in the other. The crimson embers lit up his hazel eyes that were focused squarely on reading. The forest nightlife was active with insects and nocturnal creatures that chirped, scratched, and whistled to each other. To most people, it was a peaceful setting; however, the noise against a dark forest backdrop made Coura restless.

Finally, when the moon was high above and the coals were only faintly glowing did she decide that sleep was not going to come. As quietly as she could, Coura got up and stood beside Marcus, who didn't remove his eyes from the book.

"Can't sleep?"

"I figure there's no sense in both of us being up when I'm not meant to sleep tonight."

After a moment, he closed his book, blew out the candle, and stretched. "I'll keep you company until my mind settles."

Marcus patted the ground next to him with a tired smile and Coura took a seat. From their first meeting on the training grounds to now, she was beginning to like Marcus. He answered Will's incessant questions with patience and brought up casual conversation about the academy and mage training with Byron. Meanwhile, Coura kept to herself at the front of the group but listened with interest.

Every time he talks, it feels genuine. Even his expressions aren't covered like everyone else's at the palace.

"Why do you want to be a general?" she asked suddenly.

"Well, that's a little out of the blue," Marcus glanced sideways at her.

"You spent a good part of the day explaining your position and the army but never told us about yourself."

He chuckled awkwardly, the first sign of discomfort he had shown. "I guess I think of this assignment as more of a duty than a leisure venture."

"What do you mean?"

After a moment of thought, Marcus smiled to himself. "This is the first time I have been outside of the capital city. When I was recommended to accompany you all, I think they could tell I was eager to see the country."

"Wow, I shouldn't be surprised, though. I can't imagine they let very many leaders within the army leave without a good reason."

"That, and I'm leaving my father behind."

"Oh?"

"Actually, he was the one who convinced the council to send me."

"Really?"

"After all, he *is* one of the oldest generals." His eyes danced as he smiled at her expression.

"Your *father* is a general! Why didn't you say so before?"

"I was trying to be mindful of my duty. This journey is interesting. I'm learning so much, but the council warned me about sharing my position. Just in case anything were to happen…"

"I can understand," Coura said thoughtfully. There was a long pause before either one of them said anything else. "You didn't mention our spar," she told him shyly.

Again, he shrugged. "Should I have?"

"No. I mean, I don't care what you do," she said more harshly than she intended.

"Oh." He yawned and stood up. "I suppose I should get some rest." As he settled himself in the grass across the firepit, Coura turned her face upward to the stars glimmering above.

"Hey," Marcus whispered. She looked over to where he lay staring at her with a half asleep expression. "About yesterday, I didn't want to make you look bad by explaining how you cheated. You have to promise me a rematch sometime, though."

"What? Why you..." He was already asleep when she growled back, so she turned her attention to the stars. After a while, Coura chuckled to herself. "Fine, I promise."

1

The majority of their return to the academy went as expected. Byron made sure to take the same route used to get them to the capital because it kept them away from any towns. Although he did not say anything to Coura and the two boys, Byron expected they shared his caution. After breakfast, they set out in silence.

Not only are we carrying important documents straight from the council and the king, but they also sent a second-class soldier along with us. If that doesn't raise suspicions, well, I guess I would be losing my touch. I also have had a strange feeling since we left the palace, almost as if there's a magical presence in the air. I can't pinpoint a location, though. The thought of being followed concerned Byron, but he wasn't truly worried yet. *We are about a day and a half away from the academy. If we can make it to familiar borders by nightfall, I think we'll be all right.*

"What's wrong?" As usual, Will noticed when something was bothering any of them.

Byron relaxed and put his thoughts in the back of his mind to answer him. "Nothing. I've just been thinking," he said, deciding it was not worth getting the boy worked up. Will didn't look convinced but did not question him further.

The beautiful setting of the shades of green, colorful flowers scattered like gems around the forest, and happily chirping creatures helped lighten Byron's mood throughout the morning. Will made the group stop a few times to collect samples of plants and other substances he spotted with a keen eye, but other than that.

they were making good time. Now, while Marcus and Coura nibbled on their lunches nearby, Byron knelt beside Will in the tall grass.

"What is it this time?"

Without breaking his concentration, the boy explained. "It's a fungus called the 'earth-shroom.' All around us is this wild grass and lemongrass. For some reason, it only grows in the shade of lemongrass, which makes it pretty rare. I've never been able to work with it much since I can't stock enough of it."

"I see. Lucky for you then." With the other two out of earshot, Byron decided to confront Will with a thought. "I need to ask you something," he said in a lowered voice.

The boy caught on to his serious tone and looked up with the same worry as this morning. "What is it, Master Byron?"

To ease some of his concern, Byron gave him a small smile. "Will, please just call me Byron. I wanted to ask what you will be doing when we reach the academy. That will be the end of our journey together, after all."

"Oh, of course..." Will went silent as he finished up with the sample. "I guess I'll continue exploring these forests in the north. After all, there's no reason for me to stay, what with the light mages." He let out a dry chuckle that made Byron wince.

"I suppose this was one of the first times you have traveled with other people."

"Actually, it is the first. I mean, no one really *needs* an herbalist with them. Besides, my duty is to my research. I only slow us down."

Now Byron sensed how disheartened Will was about traveling alone. "There's no reason to feel down," he put a hand on the boy's shoulder in reassurance, "After all, it's the innovation and dedication of researchers that leads to so many beneficial things."

"I guess you're right."

An idea came to Byron then, and he got to his feet. "With that being said, I am concerned with the idea of you traveling alone without any defensive skills. Perhaps there is something we can do at the academy, maybe ask about combat lessons."

His suggestion must have been what Will wanted to hear for he showed surprise, then elation. "Oh, Mas— I mean, Byron, that would be fantastic!"

As Byron helped the boy to his feet, he caught Marcus and Coura staring at them. "Let's continue," he said loud enough for all of them to hear.

With Will in an obviously better mood, he returned to his normal, talkative self. Marcus happened to be the first to ask about his samples, which led Will into a lecture on each one's properties. Byron cast Marcus a look of pity, and the boy responded with a rueful smile, then hurried his pace to where Coura led several steps ahead.

"You're unnaturally quiet." She only shrugged and continued to scan the woods ahead. "Is there something on your mind?" He knew her too well to know there was, but he didn't care to force it out of her.

Perhaps it's Marcus. I thought I recognized him, but it took me a while to remember I pulled her out of a scramble with him a few days ago. She probably doesn't trust him as a soldier either. Given time, he figured she would warm up to him like she did with Will.

"Coura, can you hand me something to eat? I'm starving," Will exclaimed from behind. They all slowed their pace, and she removed a wrapped sandwich from her pack while Marcus rubbed his eyes.

"Tired?" Byron asked the assistant general.

"A little. Not used to keeping watch is all, but I'll be fine. I'm surprised Coura's still standing. She's the one who has been up every night."

During the first evening, Byron woke at dawn to find Coura taking his shift, claiming he needed the rest. At first, he was flattered, but every night since she had done the same thing because of restlessness. He never knew her to skimp on sleep, but her quiet and reserved behavior made more sense.

"It's because she hates the woods," Will said in between bites, surprising the rest.

Marcus tilted his head at her. "What?"

"No, I don't," she snapped at him.

Will blinked in surprise. "Really? It sure seems that way."

"Why do you keep bringing that up?" she asked with more curiosity and less fiercely.

"It's like I said before. You have not slept well except at the palace and are still glaring into the trees like you're worried something will jump out."

Byron cast her a curious glance, waiting for Coura to yell again, as was her nature.

Instead, she looked up to the sky with a mixture of exasperation and uneasiness. "I don't hate the woods. It's just that every time we've been out here something ... doesn't feel right. I don't know how to explain it."

She shook her head, and Byron's heart sank. *Just as I am unable to pinpoint what I'm sensing, she knows there is something too. If it's bothering her this much, it is strong and most likely not peaceful.*

He met her eyes seriously. "Is it magic you're sensing? I have felt something as well since we left Verona, but I haven't been able to tell exactly what it is." They fell silent, the three looked to him with anxious expressions.

Byron closed his eyes and tried once more to sense that feeling. "Coura, I'm trying to see if I can identify where it is coming from and if it's hostile toward us. Do the same," he ordered. A familiar "tickling" sensation met his mind. *There it is. Now, let's see if I can get a read on it.*

Probing magical energies was like walking down a road and looking a stranger up and down; however, only those with a large center of power can sense others' energies in detail. This meant there was always a chance they could be noticed by someone, for good or for bad. In several instances, Byron was needed to see if a mage was alive, where they were, or if a spy was among a group. There was always the chance *he* could be probed, but it was extremely rare. As far as he knew, there were less than a dozen mages in Asteom with this ability, Coura being the youngest. More importantly, one could tell instantly if the power held a demonic presence. Dark energy felt heavy, like breathing in humid air, and very active, like sparks of lightning.

Byron caught the energy but as usual could not figure out where it was centered. What worried him most was that it felt entirely new. Unlike every other mage's energy, it was very light and cool, almost the opposite of a demon's. Of course, it was also extremely faint, which did not help anything. Finally, he opened his eyes. Marcus watched the trees around them with a hand on his sword.

"What did you find?" Will asked hesitantly.

"I'm not sure. Coura?"

"I don't like it," she answered, still glancing up at the sky.

Byron chewed on his lip for a moment. "It was too faint for me to trace, but I did not sense any malice. It's definitely not a demonic creature, which is good news for us."

Now Coura met his eyes again and shook her head. "I don't like it. It felt wrong. I can't explain it, but it clashed against my own energies."

"I never heard of anything like that," he said with uncertainty.

His student nodded. "You are right too. I can't get a center location, but I'm almost certain it's watching us through what *we* can sense."

Byron bit off a frustrated curse and scowled in thought. *Coura's probing skills are better than mine, so if it's bothering her this much, it must be serious. We had better hurry. Although, I wonder if this mage plans on stepping in before we get to the academy. There's no doubt it's watching us, but why? I would rather not take any chances out here where we're alone.*

"What will we do?" Marcus asked tensely.

Perhaps we can divert the attention elsewhere. I know there's a main road leading from Fester to East Hoover, and it's only a day's trip away. It might be best to add a detour. Besides, I've got a friend I've been meaning to see there. If anything, I'm just being overly cautious. Better to arrive later than expected than not at all.

"I think I have a plan. It might take us a little longer to get to the academy, though," Byron said at last, keeping his tone casual. "We are changing route to Fester. It's a day south from here, but it has a main road leading to the academy. You may not like it, but I propose we travel straight there. We will get a room at an inn, then head out the next day."

Marcus nodded in agreement. "We'll have eyes on us. No one would dare try anything in a highly populated city, and if they do, I know we have soldiers posted."

"Exactly. Now, let's get moving."

* * *

They made it to Fester around dawn the following morning. The thought of an unknown threat isolating them in the forest acted as motivation to pick up their normal pace. Coura was exhausted yet somehow unable to sit still until Byron picked out a decently sized inn near the edge of the city. The whole trek, she had felt anxious.

Part of me dislikes the idea of being watched by someone, or something, we can't identify. I would rather make a break for the academy or go after it than run and hide. But the other part... She shuddered. *This energy, I* hate *it! It feels as though my blood is boiling when I sense it.*

Thankfully, the friendly, plump innkeeper was so charmed by Byron's incessive complimenting that she gave them the largest room with two beds and promised lunch on her.

As Coura stared out the window, again eyeing the trees in the distance, she began to relax. Shopkeepers were opening their doors, wagons and horses noisily made their way across town, and men yawned and grumbled to one another on their way to work. Just knowing they were around other people made them all feel safer, and soon Coura stopped sensing that horrifically strange presence.

In another few minutes, she yawned and sat on the edge of her bed. Marcus and Will set up their blankets and sleeping packs on the floor as soon as they entered the room, leaving Byron and Coura with their own beds. Evidently, they figured out if it came to fighting a mage, Byron and Coura would need every bit of strength just in case. It didn't bother her any.

Byron entered carrying a large bundle of what smelled like sausage and pastry. He set it on the table to the left of the door. "All right," he kicked the door closed and fastened the lock, "I mentioned we would be resting all day, and the kind lady offered us a gift. Sleep as long as you like today. We'll plan on heading out tomorrow morning, unless plans change."

"What do you mean if plans change?" Marcus asked suspiciously. Perhaps it was lack of sleep and energy, but this was the first time Coura had noticed Marcus taking on his role as their guard.

Her teacher shook his head and laid on the bed. "There's a chance our unidentified follower may make a move before we leave. There is also a chance we may need to stay here another night to recover. Plans *do* change. That's a good thing for a general to know."

Byron's frankness was a sure sign he was tired, but thankfully Marcus only said, "I see." It didn't take any of them long after their heads met the pillows to begin catching up on some sleep.

* * *

Coura woke at some point in the afternoon, relieved by the lack of odd energies, and scarfed down a few of the treats in the innkeeper's bundle. Marcus soon followed, then Will. They ate in silence before returning to their beds to rest with full stomachs.

The next morning, Coura was in a half-awake state when the sun peered through the only window in the room. She smiled to herself and pulled the blankets tighter. She didn't know how long she had been in bed, but no one else was making a move to rise. *Perhaps I had better enjoy this comfort before the others get up.*

118

Finally, she stretched and pulled back the blankets. *If we're to be on the road soon, I'd at least like to wash up and eat, in case Byron hurries us,* she thought as she rubbed her eyes. However, when she looked around the room, Coura found herself alone. None of their belongings were packed, and there was a scrap of paper on the table beside a wrapped meal and small bag.

Coura,

It's about noon now. Will left to visit some of the shops in town earlier, and Marcus wanted to see some friends stationed here. It looks like we'll be leaving tomorrow morning. I am going to pay an old friend a visit at Wilker's Tavern at the other end of town and see what information I can gather about this area. You're free to do as you please for the rest of the day, but please *meet back here around sundown or come find me.*

—Byron

Coura left the note on the table and picked up the meat pie. She ate it quickly and glanced out the window. *I can't believe it's already after noon. I guess I needed sleep more than I thought.*

After dressing and rinsing her face off in a basin someone left in the room, Coura pulled her hair back and grabbed the small bag filled with a dozen coins. It wasn't much, but it was enough to purchase a trinket or jewelry if she liked it.

Fester reminded her of Verona in size. It was expansive with a main road consisting of shops, then plenty of back trails leading to homes and farms near the outside of the city. In her leisure time, Coura tried going into every shop. Along the way, she purchased roasted nuts from a bakery and donated the rest of her money to a street performer who juggled knives, then threw them all at marked targets, including one just above his assistant's head. Although she couldn't understand how someone learned to play with weapons instead of wielding them, it entertained her nonetheless.

As the sun was beginning to fade and the sky filled with orange and red, Coura made her way back to the inn. Byron must have had the innkeeper replace their original package, for there was fresh food available when she got back. Will was the only one in the room, and he was already munching on a piece of dried jerky. They greeted each other before diving into the savory meats and pies. Will elaborately told her all about his adventure in Fester while she summed up her day in a few sentences.

"Did you make it to the potion and herbal shop? That was my favorite one! I'm sure you would like their flowers. They're all for decoration, which is why they are arranged so pretty."

Coura shook her head and rose to light the candles. At first, she thought of simply doing it herself with her power, but ultimately decided it would be better not to give off any of her energies and instead reached for the matchbox sitting next to the food. "It's well after sundown. I wonder where they could be?"

Will waved a hand in dismissal. "I wouldn't worry. Marcus said he was with some soldiers he used to train with, and I trust Byron is all right too."

"Yeah, I guess," she said but wasn't convinced. Outside, the sounds from the main street died down, and the sky was dark.

"Would you like to see some of the books I bought? They're probably not what you are interested in..."

"Sure."

He looked at Coura with surprise. "Really, you would?" Even as he spoke, Will dug out three books from his own pack.

As he explained each one and what information it held, Coura's mind wandered elsewhere. *Where could they be? Surely Byron didn't spend all day at a tavern just to gather information, although he did say he was meeting with an old friend. On the other hand, I still don't fully trust Marcus. I would like to, but if anything happened, I don't know if he'd be all right.*

"Coura?"

"Huh?"

Will was staring at her, his finger on a section of one chapter. "Is everything OK?"

"I think we should look for them," she said at last and got to her feet. Reluctantly, Will put his book away and followed her out of the room.

"I think you're overreacting. Don't you trust Byron?" he asked without hiding his annoyance. Coura stopped just before the door outside and spun on Will.

"You think I don't *trust* him? I'm his student, the one who has worked with him for years. So, excuse *me* for being the most concerned. If you want to stay in the room and shut yourself away, then go ahead. It's not like you and your useless books would be any help." She stormed outside, leaving Will gaping in the hall.

* * *

The tavern Byron mentioned happened to be the farthest building across town, nearly against the woods beyond. Coura tried to ignore her frustration with Will and told herself she would deal with that after she knew everyone was safe.

At the moment, she stood at the bottom of the path leading to the tavern, worried at what she would find inside, for the outside disgusted her. Firstly, the strong smell of livestock mixed with ale and sweat made the dinner in her stomach turn. Secondly, the homely men and unseemly women parading themselves around the building did anything but make her want to go in. How anyone could stand to be near the place for so long, she had no clue.

And this is just the outside...

After her senses adjusted, Coura prepared to approach from the main road when a glint of light nearby caught her attention. She paused, pressing herself into the shadow of the last shop on the road. The shine came from a soldier's suit of armor as two guardsmen stood under the light of a street lantern across from her hiding spot. One laughed while the other hushed him impatiently. Coura stretched her ears to catch their conversation.

"You crack me up. Why'd a general lie to us?" the one who laughed asked, a little too loud to be sober.

"Will you hush up! All I'm saying is *our* orders come straight from the capital. Sure, young Marcus might be able to restrain 'em, but I'd rather not risk losing this opportunity to get promoted."

The other soldier gave an ugly snort. "You think too much, that's what *I'm* saying. I don't care whether we follow the kid's orders or not. I also don't care none about promotions and such. Let's just arrest the old man and be done with it."

Coura was on edge from the moment they mentioned Marcus. Now, her heart beat too loud in her ears. *Arrest Byron? What are they saying? Why would they arrest a messenger? There's something not right here, and I'd better warn Byron and see if I can find Marcus.*

122

Silently, Coura slipped back onto the road and approached the tavern as casually as she could muster, ignoring the uncomfortable stares and words of those outside.

8

Although Byron wasn't one for visiting taverns while traveling for business, he always cherished his visits to Fester for the chance to come to this particular place. He spent all afternoon slowly building up a comfortable drunkenness while catching up with some familiar faces.

When he first had arrived, Byron recognized a farmer who he had become acquainted with several years earlier. The man's youngest son accidentally set their barn on fire when he discovered his ability to use dark magic but did not tell anyone. In fact, that was the example Byron used days ago for Coura. He was sent to take the boy to the academy and to ease the burden on his family by explaining the situation. In this case, the farmer and his wife had three other sons, so it was exciting for one to become a mage once they understood his power.

When he joined the farmer that afternoon, he learned the four sons had turned into five with a youngest daughter. He filled Byron in on the boy's position as a mage stationed in Fester as well as the family's interest in their youngest daughter's potential for magic. Soon enough, they were joined by his mage son and two others Byron recognized from years back.

By the time they all had left for supper, Byron was ready to eat as well. A young barmaid brought him some of the tavern's stew and bread, and of course more ale, before chatting with him about the area's prosperity. Although she claimed not to know much, the woman was very good at collecting gossip in her position. Byron recognized several names and learned many more. Overall, Fester was well-off, but rumors circled of livestock being spooked by creatures in the woods.

"That's why the soldiers are out at night too. Usually one or two before, but now at least six," she said quietly. "I haven't seen anything, but I'm always here. You should try talking to the guardsmen when they come in."

He thanked the woman and ate his meal with care. *I would rather avoid the soldiers stationed here at the moment. After all, my first task is to return these papers to the academy. There's a risk in too many people knowing we're here, but if anything were to happen, I'd rather they do know. Besides, I would hate to raise suspicions with Marcus.*

That morning, he and Byron were up and ate together before the assistant general requested they remain one more day. Lucky for him, Byron felt the same, but he asked why.

"I have some friends stationed here, soldiers I trained and trained with. Also, I think it's important for them to know that we stopped here and why. Don't worry, I won't go into detail. I plan to tell them we did this as a precaution in case anyone was trailing us, that's all. I would hate for you or me to get in trouble for taking extra days to bring these documents to the academy."

I do like him, Byron reflected as he cleared his bowl. *He will grow into an honest man and a good commander, I'm sure.*

What he neglected to tell any of the others in his company was his reason for visiting Fester specifically. Later that evening, after sharing a few more drinks with new and old friends, Byron made his way to the back of the building as the main area filled.

Half of the common room held tables and benches with the bar at one end. About a third of the room was left open for musicians to play and dancers or performers to entertain. This

126

evening, a lively band with various instruments were barely heard over the chatter, laughter, and attempts at singing over the music. It was a good time for Byron to consult with one of the tavern's famous backroom ladies.

Several attractive women offered their wares for the right price in reserved spaces. Guests paid for their time beforehand and for their privacy, meaning the women heard things not intended to be repeated outside of the room. He hoped he would be able to pick up some information from a reliable source.

He knocked on the final door of the row while the other open ladies gave him looks of mock sadness at their rejection. Byron only smiled warmly and waited. Meanwhile, a muscular man watched him from nearby. It was protocol to have someone keeping an eye on the … assets. The door, painted with a gold star in the center, opened, and Byron couldn't help but grin as the woman's jaw dropped.

"Well, I'll be. It's been too long, Byron!"

"It has, Cintra."

As she ushered him inside, he caught her nod to the guard, who caught the message and left them alone. When the door closed, his longtime friend turned with arms wide open. He embraced her, trying not to think of her nearly exposed breasts in the tight gown, and took a seat at one of the chairs.

The room was rather small and contained only a bed, including a colorful canopy, a table with burning incense, various accessories, and a pot of water. Cintra spread herself out on the bed, laying on her side and eyeing him with interest.

It was difficult for Byron not to get aroused by her, especially since he was inebriated. Her long blonde hair was half tied up and left a trail down her back. While she had too much make-up on for his liking, it made her blue eyes stand out even in the dimly lit room, her cheeks appear flushed, and her lips a bright red. As he always noticed, her low-cut dress exposed plenty of skin. The skirt of her dress was pulled back to show much of her legs.

Despite appearances, the woman showed no desire to seduce him, which was exactly how he liked it. After all, they had grown up together. At one point he even encouraged her to pursue this profession. She loved "performing" but was also good at something else.

Somewhere in her ancestry was light blood so unique it showed her visions of a future that might come to pass. No other person, as far as Byron knew, had this ability, not even the most powerful light mages, which made her valuable. They were young when Cintra began having visions. She was afraid, but he promised to help. Soon some of the visions came true, and that scared her almost too much to bear. However, Byron stood by her side until he was forced to deal with his own developing powers. At the academy, he urged her to join him, but she refused.

"If anyone found out, I could be taken away or made to serve for the rest of my life. I would rather cope with these visions than become someone's slave."

Years later, Byron learned of her position at this tavern. When he visited then, he was happy to know she had taught herself to control her visions by channeling them into a source. The first time she showed him, she pulled out a violet gemstone and focused on that. He sensed the energies at work, and she successfully predicted a small part of his future.

"Of course, it's not a hundred percent accurate, but it is something to go off of," she had told him the first time. Every now and then she accepted payment for reading guests' futures, earning her title as "Cintra the Visionary."

"Well, what brings the famous teacher to me?" she asked with narrowed eyes.

Byron feigned innocence. "I can't come visit you every so often without suspicion?"

Cintra laughed, a rich sound compared to the grumbling and singing in the common room. "If that's all it is, I would love to catch up!"

So they talked for a while, trading stories of events in the academy, Fester, and all over the region. "I'm told there are more creatures lurking in the woods," Byron finally said after a while, when matters turned more serious.

Cintra nodded slowly. "It's true. Most men here will act tough about it, but I'll be honest, it worries me."

"Have you..."

This time she shook her head. "I tried seeing ahead, but all I get is darkness, and Byron, it frightens me. I've *never* not been able to see visions. Whatever this is ... I can think of only two things." She bit her lip in thought.

"I'm worried too, but I trust your sight. You know that, I hope," he said in a reassuring manner.

A little light returned to her eyes, and she nodded. "Of course."

"What do you think?"

With a sigh, Cintra shifted her sitting position. "Number one, there will be dark energies involved. Perhaps so much that my vision can't make sense of it all. Either that or my light blood won't be able to sense past it."

"What is number two?"

"I think it's more likely because the future is so muddled at this point. Remember those times when I couldn't make heads or tails of what I saw? It might be like that, only on a larger scale. I don't know how else to explain it."

"I think I get the idea," he said slowly.

"I can try again. Maybe with you here I will see something else."

"I'm up for it if you are," he answered with a hopeful expression.

Cintra bent over and pulled out a sack from under the bed. From it, she removed a crystal orb and some jewelry. She told him once how the metal and stones of the bracelets and earrings helped enhance details, and he couldn't see any reason to doubt her. After putting them on, she held the orb with one hand and took one of his in the other. Immediately, Byron sensed her light energies at work, their frailness reminding him of a spider weaving its web. It was over in a minute. Cintra released his hand and rubbed a temple.

He tried to be patient while she relaxed again. "What did you see?"

With weary eyes, she looked down at the floor. "It's still hazy, but I was able to make out a few things surrounding you. There was a castle, and an army..."

"An army?"

"Yes. Their bodies shone in the light. There was also an *angel*," she spoke just above a whisper.

Now Byron was surprised. "An angel? What do you mean?"

"Exactly that. A person with wings flying through the sky. I think there was just one, but there might have been another."

"An angel," he breathed, unable to comprehend Cintra's vision.

"There's more. You were covered with blood and appeared frightened." She visibly shuddered.

Byron quickly moved to her side on the bed and put an arm around her shoulders. "I know it must worry you, but thank you for trying."

She smiled up at him and put a hand to his cheek. "Of course, my friend. I just can't stand to see anything happen to those I care about."

"You and me both."

They sat like that, enjoying each other's company, until Cintra went to the door and left. She returned shortly with a bottle of wine. "Now that the business is out of the way, why don't we relax a bit, hmm?"

"I'd like that," Byron eagerly grinned.

* * *

The inside of Wilken's Tavern was utter chaos to Coura, who immediately felt drowned in a sea of drunks, half-naked women, and smoke. In the back of her mind, she hoped Will was still at the inn and would not follow. She could barely tolerate this atmosphere, let alone keep track of him in it.

First thing's first, I need to blend in and see where he could be. There were barmaids who carefully weaved through the traffic, and she grabbed a mug of beer off one's tray while she was occupied with a perverted older man.

Try as she might, Coura couldn't avoid staring at some of the faces around her. There were many soldiers in uniform, which put her on edge, though they were all in a giddy mood and paid her no attention. She could not imagine how anyone heard themselves, let alone others, amid the noise. For a while, she wandered around trying to make out Byron. It wasn't until she reached the farthest end where there was an open space for dancing did she recognize Marcus. As she might have expected, he was surrounded by a group of younger soldiers, each with a woman in their arms. The group was attempting to dance, but to her, they appeared to be flailing or jumping around.

Without bringing too much attention to herself, she slipped up next to Marcus and grabbed his arm. He blinked at her for a moment before smiling gingerly as he recognized her. Coura nearly gagged at the smell of ale heavy on his breath.

"I didn't think I'd see you here!" He put an arm around her waist to pull her in close.

"It's time to go," she said in a flat, unamused tone.

Marcus counted his fingers. "What? We can't leave yet! It's only…"

"We don't have time for this," Coura cut in impatiently and tried to pull him back; however, she underestimated his physical strength. He pushed her into his chest and brought his face close to hers.

"What's the rush?" His breath was hot on her face.

"Stop it," she warned through clenched teeth as her cheeks began to flush at his lack of personal space. Although she tried to push away, Marcus held her firm and even seemed to be moving in closer. Her heartbeat picked up. Suddenly, Coura remembered the mug in her hand and smiled as she knew how to get them out.

Fine, have it your way. She let out a whoop in his face, which startled him enough to release his hold on her. As the others around looked on, she yelled, "Cheers!" In their drunken stupor, anyone who heard her yell took a swig of their drink. In that moment, Coura took advantage of the noise to bring her mug up and crack it against the side of Marcus's head. It knocked him out cold, and he fell face-first onto the floor. Although they didn't really see or hear the crash, those around them looked on with amusement and concern.

"Looks like someone can't handle his drinks," she shouted and was rewarded with their laughter.

"Best to get 'im off the floor 'or somebody trips," one of the soldiers slurred nearby.

"Yes, sir," she mock-saluted him, which earned her a wink and grin. However, upon trying to lift his body, Coura found she was too weak to do much. "I don't know if anyone here is strong enough to help me…" She glanced down at Marcus, then to the soldiers helplessly.

A soldier, appearing older than anyone else in their group, came to her side. "Aye, I can't leave a pretty lady like yourself to carry his drunk ass around." She overexaggerated her thanks and put herself under one of Marcus's arms. Together, they somehow managed to lug him to the entrance where he began to come to.

Through grumbles, Marcus's legs started working again. Quickly, Coura waved off the other man. "I think I can handle it from here," she told him honestly.

"Good luck to you then," he waved and faded into the crowd inside.

"W-what are we … Coura? You … you *hit* me!"

"Yeah, yeah. Keep moving," she ordered as they left the building.

Finally, we're getting somewhere.

As they approached the main road, she saw someone running down to meet them and recognized Will immediately with a sinking heart. "Now what," she muttered.

"Coura, there you are!" He spoke in a hushed tone and carried his pack.

"Will, what's going on? Why do you have your bag?"

It took him a moment to catch his breath and recognize Marcus slouched up against her. "Is he all right?"

"Will! What are you *doing* here?"

"Right," he shook his head and backtracked. "I started going upstairs after you left and sat in the room for a little while, then I decided I was going to find you. As soon as I went near the exit, I heard the innkeeper talking with somebody. She mentioned that Byron was at the tavern and didn't know when he would be back. The man said they could just go get him there. It sounded shady, so I hurried to the room again to try and figure out what to do. I could only carry my things, so I packed them up and left to find you without the innkeeper noticing." Will was nearly hysterical and continued on about his concerns.

Coura's head hurt. What was worse was that, away from the many people, she felt a slight tingle of that familiar presence. *If Byron and Marcus would have kept their word in the first place, we would be together. I have to think! If what I heard matches up with Will's story, the city guards will be searching for Byron. I'd rather them not find us, especially if he is in no better state than Marcus.* As if sensing her thoughts, the soldier groaned and mumbled about returning to the festivities.

"Shut up," she snapped at them both, and, luckily, they obeyed. "We can't stay at the inn. There's no time to explain, but the city guards are looking for Byron, probably to arrest him for leaving the route or something. I think it would be smarter to camp outside of the city."

"Aren't we avoiding the woods?" Will put in. "Besides, we don't know for sure if they are going to arrest him. I'm sure if we mentioned our situation, they would listen."

"They are!" Marcus, suddenly alert, blurted out.

"What?"

He nodded lazily. "I heard it from my comrades in there. The council told 'em if Byron runs away, they were supposed to lock him up and deliver the documents without question."

"What!" both Coura and Will exclaimed.

"Mmhm, but don't worry. I already told 'em I'd be with you guys. They're listening to me." His head drooped, and Coura was suddenly struggling to support him.

She smacked the back of his head with her hand. "Wake *up*, Marcus! They *are* going to arrest him. I overheard the soldiers say so, even though it goes against your orders." He continued to ignore her but put more weight on his own legs, which was enough at the moment.

Coura glanced at Will, who appeared clueless and looked to her for a decision. "Listen," she started, "we do not have time to stand here and argue. Even if nothing were to happen, I'd rather be safe and out of the way. Follow me ... over there."

She pointed with one hand toward a spot at the edge of the forest just beyond the tavern. Together, they dragged Marcus's now limp body across the clearing, past the building, and into the surrounding trees. Once they passed by a couple of wider trees, Coura was relieved to see the space open up into a secluded, grassy area just big enough for all four of them to fit snugly.

"Here, this will do," she ordered. While Will attempted to set Marcus down without harming him, she dropped her burden and let him slouch onto the ground. She surveyed the clearing, leaving Will to flip the soldier onto his back and adjust his limbs into a more comfortable position that would not result in stiff muscles later. Once he was finished, she grabbed Will by the shoulder and began making her way back to town.

"What are you doing? We can't just leave him," he protested.

Coura let go of him as soon as they were in the clearing, a solid plan formulating. "I need you to go back to the inn, pack the rest of our bags, and bring them to where we put Marcus. Make sure to load Byron's things first, then Marcus's. My stuff won't be missed, but the documents are our priority. If anyone finds them..."

He nodded, catching the message. "What will you do?"

"I'm going to find Byron. From what I heard, the soldiers are looking to go after him tonight."

"This late?"

It was her turn to nod before urging him to hurry. Without another word, they parted ways.

9

As she searched Wilken's Tavern once again for her mentor, Coura forced herself to breathe and keep moving lest she break down altogether. *Where could he be? I doubt he would leave, but Will can find me if he returns to the inn. I can't even think about if they have caught him already. Then again, there would be word among the guards if that had happened.*

For how late it was this evening, there were about as many people as there were when she had left, and all still as active as she had last left them. It was obvious to her, after one more glance around the room, that her teacher was not in the common room. That was when she noticed several doors at the far end of the building that she had not paid any attention to earlier. Upon further inspection, Coura recognized the women waiting outside.

There's no way Byron would go in there ... would he? I checked everywhere else in here, so I guess I have no choice.

Coura counted ten doors. Six of them had women standing outside showing themselves off. After waiting for a little while, three men left three of the rooms, leaving the last door on the end. She also noted the muscular guard keeping watch over the rooms. It took even longer for his attention to divert to a couple of younger men roughhousing, and when he turned to break them apart, she hurried to the door. By some fortune, it was unlocked.

She slipped inside unnoticed and found Byron alone with a woman in the cramped, heavily scented room. He was lying facedown on the full-sized bed with his shirt off while the woman, who was actually quite beautiful, rubbed his back. Coura coughed at the incense filling up the space and startled the woman.

"Who are you? What are you doing in here?" her high-pitched voice squealed with fright.

Instead of blowing up at the woman like she felt like doing, Coura took a deep breath, glared at the woman, and spoke slowly, biting off every word. "I'm here for him, so if you know what's good for you, you had better sit and stay quiet until we are gone."

"N-no," the woman stepped closer to Byron and instinctively put a hand on his shoulder.

He groaned and lifted his head, blinking at the woman with an expression that was not quite awake or sober. "Cintra, what's wrong?"

They both ignored him. "I won't let you hurt him," the woman said with more strength. "If you come any closer, I'll scream!"

"Hurt him? I'm here to *help* him!"

"Coura?" Byron sat up, face very red, and rubbed his eyes.

"We have to go," she said and moved to grab him. The woman still didn't budge, even reaching to push Coura away.

I don't have time for this, she thought urgently. Instead of fighting back, she used her slimmer size to duck under the woman's outstretched arm and slide behind her, then she twisted around to kick her backside. With an "oof" the woman fell forward onto the floor. Now that she could, Coura grabbed one of Byron's arms and heaved him into a sitting position.

"We have to go," was all she said through her teeth.

"What are you doing here?" he asked with annoyance, but he let her pull him to his feet. To her relief, only his shirt was missing, and she located it on the small table next to several strange objects. He continued to chastise her for the interruption but made no effort to keep her away as she helped him put his shirt on. Once he was decent, Coura prepared to pull him toward the door when they heard a soft whimper.

"Byron," the woman cried gently in a wavering voice from where she remained on the floor. He seemed to notice her then and attempted to go to her. However, his body did not cooperate, and he ended up wobbling before clutching onto Coura. She bit back her venomous insults as she directed him to the door, now blocked by the woman.

"Move," Coura ordered firmly with the last of her sanity.

"I won't!"

"Are you all right?" Byron asked her through a groan.

A curt knock on the door made Coura jump and start to panic. As the woman got up and put a hand on the doorknob, she glanced back at the two of them.

"Please," Coura begged, hoping to convey her helplessness both in her voice and expression, "don't tell them we're here."

Despite their position, the woman's eyes softened, and she gave Coura a nod before opening the door. As she did so, Coura shoved Byron back by the bed out of the doorway's line of sight into the room.

"What're you doing here?" he asked again before she shushed him to watch the woman. She couldn't make out who was at the door and why over the dim lighting and noise in the common room. It took them less than a moment to talk before the woman closed the door slowly and turned to them.

"Why are the city's soldiers looking for Byron?" she asked. It was evident then by the sincerity and concern in her voice that the woman had some sort of personal connection to Byron, meaning that Coura could relax for the moment.

"It's a long story," she sighed with relief at the woman's co-operation.

"I know what you must be thinking. We, Byron and I, we grew up together. He is a dear friend to me, and I would never rat him out. He came here to catch up with me, that's all."

Although Coura could tell she was hiding something, there was no doubt in the woman's expression of her care for Byron. "We are heading back to the Magic Arts Academy from Verona to deliver some important documents. There was something following us in the woods, so we decided to spend some time here and take the main road back to East Hoover. Apparently, some people aren't happy we left the path and think Byron is committing treason by running away. Although, I'm fairly sure they just want us out of the picture so decisions can go their way."

"I see," the woman answered with wide eyes. "The soldiers were told to keep him here to make people think he had abandoned his post!"

Whatever Coura was about to say turned to nothing at the woman's words. *I didn't even think about them keeping us here to make it seem as if Byron had abandoned his position. Byron said he and the council did not appear to leave on good terms, and I wouldn't put it past Hernan to sneak around like that either.*

The woman took advantage of that moment to move to Byron's side and shake his now-limp body. "I might have given him a little too much wine, but you two can leave through the back door so they don't see you. What do you plan to do once you're outside? Actually, never mind. It's probably better I don't know where he went."

With a groan, Byron raised his head and complained about Coura again before the woman had him on his feet and moving toward the wall opposite the bed. She pulled back the heavy curtain covering its entirety to reveal another door.

"This is what we use if there is an emergency or we need some fresh air. Of course, it's only for us normally. Since I'm on the end, it won't be that long of a walk with him. Turn right and follow the hallway to the outside exit. You will be at the back of the tavern." She forcefully removed Byron's arm from her shoulders and transferred his weight to Coura.

"Thank you," Coura found herself saying with surprise. The woman gave her a relieved smile.

"By the way, my name is Cintra." She glanced at Byron with sympathy. "Please, take care of him. He's a good man."

"I know," Coura said awkwardly. "I'm his student, after all."

As if in recognition, Cintra's mouth fell open a bit, but she said nothing more as she ushered them into the hallway beyond and closed the door.

Once alone, Coura led Byron to the right as Cintra had instructed. The space was very dark, but Coura was able to make out walls and followed them through touch. Only moments later, as promised, they were at the exit. With her free hand, she turned the knob and kicked the door open with haste. The crisp night air felt good on Coura's body as she took in a few deep breaths of the fresh air before moving on.

After being stuffed inside the tavern for so long, she was relieved to be alone with her thoughts, and Byron's continuous grumbles. "Why'd we leave? Where's Cintra? You shouldn't have been in there." Coura knew better than to try and argue with a drunk man, so she continually apologized and pulled him along.

Since they came out through the back of the tavern, there were only storage barrels, wagons, and various supplies for the kitchen. They were also a lot closer to the woods where she had left Marcus, which was most important at the moment. Coura strained to see the open field in front of and to the side of Wilken's Tavern and scanned for Will. She hoped he had been able to grab their bags before she returned. *I'm exhausted, but if I have to help him, I guess I must.*

The made it to the trees after an agonizing amount of time due to Byron's stumbling. She pushed bush branches out of her way, not so concerned with them hitting Byron, and finally entered their clearing. Byron's bedroll was sloppily set up, but once he saw it, he pushed off of Coura, nearly knocking her over in the process, and sprawled out onto it. She rolled her shoulders to free up the tense muscles after supporting him, thankful for not having to carry any more bodies around. Marcus was snoozing where they had left him, and, after fumbling through the darkness, Coura located each of the four packs loaded with all of their belongings. Most importantly, she found the documents in Byron's bag sealed in their travel wrapping.

Thank goodness, she thought with relief that shook her entire body.

"Will, where are you?" Coura whispered into the night.

No response.

Maybe he went back to the inn, she thought with some worry as she considered the innkeeper's willingness to turn them in. A groan escaped her. She wanted nothing more than to lie down for the evening, yet her conscience would not rest until their entire group was together again. With that in mind, she began making her way through the brush.

Soon, she found herself at the edge of the woods overlooking the clearing and Fester beyond. Most of the lights in the city were out except for those lanterns lit to illuminate the main streets. A glance up at the sky told Coura it was well past midnight, probably closer to morning than she liked.

With a sigh, she took a step toward the building, intent on sneaking into the inn to see where Will might be. In the next instant, she was struck numb by an overwhelming sense of magic, the very same presence they had been trying to avoid. As her legs gave way, Coura sank to her knees and froze. There was no mistaking it as anything different, but it was terribly close. That knowledge alone terrified her stiff, though her blood hummed furiously in response.

It's here, and so close...

A sort of despair set over her mind as she wondered what she could possibly do. *There's no way I can go after it alone, and I can't move both of Byron and Marcus in time. Byron's in no shape to fight, and neither is Marcus, and Will is...*

As she spun to face the woods where she knew the mage or creature lurked, Coura's heart sank further. *What if it got Will? What if it comes for Byron and Marcus next? I have to make sure, then maybe I can lead it away from them. That's my only chance until Byron wakes up.*

Shakily, she pushed herself back to her feet, took a few deep breaths to calm her mind, then entered the forest again. She returned to their camp to grab her sword, which sat untouched in her pack during the journey until that moment, then turned to the source of that strange, unnerving energy that lingered around the entire area.

Her body was tense as she hurried without trying to make too much noise. In the quiet of the night, there were the sounds of insects to cover her tracks, which could only do so much. She did find a little luck knowing the source was definitely farther into the woods than where Byron and Marcus were sleeping. However, as Coura moved deeper, she could make out distant voices cutting through the stillness. One was a male's, the other a softer female's. They spoke back and forth too faintly to make out, but a cry carried to her with clarity.

"I don't know!"

She froze again. *That was Will's voice! Oh no, they did find him after all. Now what do I do?*

Even as she attempted to process the situation, her body involuntarily continued moving stealthily toward the voices. *Why am I still walking? I need to figure out a plan or get help instead!* She screamed at herself for ignoring logic, yet her legs would not obey. What was worse, the trembling sensation from the clashing energies became nearly unbearable until something in her center steadied her. Coura stopped shaking with fear and focused with what she could only describe as anticipation. Meanwhile, her heart drummed away and threatened to suffocate her.

At long last, she quietly peeled away a branch and stopped in a crouch to see the two owners of the voices huddled over Will. He was shrinking away from them, arms wrapped around himself and tears streaming down his cheeks. There were spots of blood covering his clothes, and his nose looked swollen.

"P-please, I t-told you..." he begged again.

From this angle, Coura could see Will perfectly now that her eyes had adjusted to the dark. It also helped that they were in another small clearing and the moonlight shone down on them. Unfortunately, she couldn't see the strangers' faces nor their bodies because of the bulky, white packs spanning the length of their backs.

"Why do you lie to us? We have seen you and the mages together," the female cooed. She knelt down in front of Will, who tried to pull away as she brushed his face with a hand. "Tell us where they are, and we will let you go. I'd hate to cause such a cute boy more trouble."

Will remained silent.

"So stubborn," the male said sarcastically with wicked amusement.

"Why do you protect them?" the woman said as she stood, all kindness gone from her voice. Still, Will did not answer.

Coura watched her with interest, noticing how the white bulks on their backs seemed to move *with* their own movements. *It's almost like they're adjusting themselves. Could they have some secret weapon? I can't fight them if they have the upper hand. Who are these people?*

In a sudden move, the male reached down and grabbed Will by the hair. Will yelped and his hands flew to the man's grip in an attempt to claw himself free. Coura could only watch as he was lifted effortlessly to meet the man's eyes.

"Where are they," he said in a deathly serious tone.

"Please," Will whimpered, a sound that broke Coura's heart.

From his other hand, the stranger called forth a flame large enough to light up the whole space. She had to look away momentarily and let her eyes adjust to the brightness. When she looked back, every thought fled her mind as she took in what the light revealed. The wrapped lumps on their backs she had thought were packs were something else entirely. The white feathers fluttered to life as if the light called them awake.

Coura heard her breath catch at the sight as a sense of awe overwhelmed her. *They're wings, actual wings. That must mean these people are angels. This can't be—no one has seen an angel in decades! Why would they be after Byron? Could they be affiliated with another country? They were supposed to be our allies, but if that were the case, why are they hurting Will?*

Amid her frantic processing, a voice rang out in her mind, louder than any other thought.

{*They are evil.*}

She blinked with uncertainty. *What? How can an angel be evil?*

{*There's no more time. Act now or let your friend die!*}

Just then, Will cried out as the man brought the flame close to his face. "Unless you *want* your eyes to be burned out, you'll tell us what you know," the male shouted ferociously.

Before Coura knew what to do, she found herself entering the clearing and approaching the strangers. "Stop," she ordered with surprising firmness, as if the voice did not belong to her. "Let him go."

The angels watched her with suspicion when she came into the clearing. Now, they looked at one another before the male dropped Will to face her. As Will gasped for air, the angel continued to hold his flame. "Who might you be?" he asked with no small hint of irritation.

"It doesn't matter," Coura heard herself say confidently. "Neither of us is worth your time, so let him go and we can be on our way."

What am I saying? I shouldn't be so easygoing with this. They're still within distance to harm Will, and there's no way I'm strong enough to fight an angel, let alone two of them! She was numb with fear before the voice returned with hot anger.

{*Enough! Quit cowering and fight!*}

Any emotions were snuffed out then by an unseen force and replaced with a sickening eagerness hiding underneath. Coura drew her sword at their glares and forced a challenging smile.

The woman took a step forward and glanced at the other. "Shall I, brother?"

He nodded. "Of course, Elsa. However, make sure to keep this one alive. I am rather interested in interrogating her once she has been beaten into submission."

The woman drew her sword, a slim, shiny blade like quicksilver, and walked casually up to meet Coura.

"Who are you looking for?" Coura ventured to ask, hoping to stall for time. While the woman answered, Coura made sure to take in all the features of her opponent. Like in any tale of the angels, the woman's hair was so white it was nearly blonde, and even in the dark she knew her eyes were most likely blue. The angel had no armor but instead wore black leather padding that covered her torso and thighs. Her "brother" had similar features, but Coura was sure he would not interfere unless necessary. This brought all of her attention to the woman in front of her.

Her limbs are exposed. Maybe I can try wearing her down before injuring them. Otherwise, her wings are an option. The thought of crimson staining the clean, unmarred feathers made Coura sad, but she knew it might save her life and Will's. *No matter the consequences, I will have to give it my all. Our lives are on the line.*

"We are looking for a dark mage named Byron Rinod. He was last seen leaving Verona and heading back to the Magic Arts Academy in East Hoover." She paused as if waiting for Coura to respond. When she didn't, the woman pointed her sword forward. "We have been told to find him through any means necessary, so your cooperation could save your life."

Coura only shook her head, keeping a sad smile. "I'm sorry to disappoint you, but I don't know anything about him."

"Then leave."

"Not as long as you're going to torture him," she jerked her chin at Will, who watched Coura with a look that told her to run.

"So be it, stranger."

10

Will could only watch helplessly as Coura stayed to defend him and began fighting with the female angel named Elsa. His head spun, mostly because of the male who had introduced himself only as "Devan" and nearly knocked him unconscious after punching him twice in the nose. He was sure it was broken but was too distracted to think about that now. Silently, he begged Coura to run, to get away. He *knew* she'd seen his expression and ignored him. Until this moment, he was skeptical that Coura would be the type of person to risk her life for someone she barely knew, but she was definitely not one to back down from a fight.

The angel leaped forward and, with a push of her wings, covered the distance between herself and Coura in seconds. Swords clashed, the sound ringing through the now-silent woods. In the dark, and with his face throbbing, Will couldn't make out too much of what was happening. What he did notice was that the angel was faster. *Much* faster. Coura blocked each blow, some sending sparks into the air, but was unable to strike herself. Will bit his lip and sent up a silent prayer.

What should I do? She looks tired. I don't think she can keep this up. I don't think I can get away, at least, not with him *watching.* He slowly looked up at the other angel standing over him, like a wolf guarding his catch. The man's face was impassive, though his eyes danced with amusement. Will hurried to follow Coura's movements again and tried to think of how he could help.

It occurred to him then that Coura hadn't used magic yet. *She's a mage like Byron, so why hasn't she done anything? That's right, she said she didn't know me. Maybe they would see the connection if she used it, or at least think she knows Byron. This isn't good...* He jumped as Coura let out a yelp when one of the blades swiped across a spot on her left arm.

The woman laughed as Coura staggered back and grabbed her bicep. The sound was equally charming and sinister. "Do you give up yet? Like I said, if you tell us what you know, we will let you both go."

"Keep him out of this," Coura shouted back. "He's got nothing to do with me!"

Elsa was silent for a moment before letting out a long "oh" and glancing to Will, who instinctively went still. "I remember now, don't you, Devan?"

"I didn't think you would remember, sister."

"Remember what?" Coura snapped.

"How foolish of me," Elsa continued. "Our leader told us the dark mage traveled with a young herbalist and provided details on his behavior..."

A shiver went down Will's spine. *Leader? How could they possibly know about me when I was only with Byron for a brief amount of time? Unless ... It had to have been someone in the palace.*

The thought was put aside as the angel went on. "He also said there was a young woman with raven hair along, but that was the only detail." Elsa casually analyzed her blade and waited for a response.

Although Will could not see Coura's reaction to the news, he expected it was similar to his own. A lack of confidence tainted the denial in her next words. "I don't know what you're talking about."

The angels laughed together in response.

* * *

How... How did they know about Will and me? Could they be bluffing, or is there someone in the capital city with other intentions? Coura tried hard to think back to the servants in the palace, but her thoughts were drowned out by the angels' harmonious amusement. She ground her teeth in frustration.

This isn't good. I am at my limit just blocking her attacks. I've never fought with anyone so swift. There's no way I can keep up with her long enough to wear her out. The angel didn't look like she had even broke a sweat, while Coura was panting. She removed her bloodied hand from where it rested on her left bicep, certain the woman had sliced through at least a quarter of her arm, and braced herself for another attack when the two sobered.

"In that case, we shall continue until you *do* remember," the female angel finally said before charging once more.

Here she comes! Again, Coura raised her sword to meet the other's blow for blow. This time, though, each strike was slower yet more powerful. It worked to her advantage since Coura's speed was decreasing far too quickly. She blocked the sword without worrying too much about it landing, but the force behind each strike drove her back step by step.

I just ... have to keep ... going...

The fear that had retreated only minutes ago was creeping up on her as her mental strength chipped away with each strike. Somehow, Coura was able to block the woman's sword during a vertical slice and hold it above her head, keeping the angel still for a little while. Their faces were mere inches away.

"Last chance," the woman said in a low voice. With a grunt, Coura pushed the sword away, stepped back, preparing to swipe horizontally at the woman's exposed mid-section, and...

What?

As her foot went back, it hit an above-ground tree root, and she found herself falling backward. There was a tree right behind her. Coura's back slammed against it. It was too late to escape. She had been caught off-guard, and her sword lowered as she fell. This gave the angel the perfect opening.

Instead of striking with the blade, the woman rushed forward, reached across the space, and grabbed Coura by the throat. In the next instant, the angel raised Coura above her head, back still pressed against the tree. Coura let go of her sword to free herself with both hands but to no avail. As if in reply, the woman dug her nails into Coura's throat. She felt a trickle of warm blood drip down her shirt and started seeing stars.

"How about now? Will you tell us what we want to know?" the angel said in that sweet voice.

"I ... don't know..." was all Coura managed to spit out in gasps. It wasn't long after that her body began to go limp and the grip on her throat tightened.

"Fine, have it your way."

That's it then... She's going to choke me... I can't...

"Elsa, hurry up!" Coura heard the male's voice, though she could not see him through the dazzling stars.

Just as she felt she was about to lose consciousness altogether, a sharp pain in her chest made her body scream, then the grip on her throat released. Coura tried gasping for air only to find herself coughing up blood in the process. Her sight returned enough for her to glance down in horror at the sword sticking out of the middle of her chest.

The female angel was returning to where the other angel and Will were. She had pinned Coura to the tree with her sword to let her bleed out, knowing she could not free herself or call out. Coura's body ached with pain and pity for Will, for how she was unable to save them both.

How could this happen…

Her hands had been weakly pulling on the hilt of the sword but finally fell limply to her side. The strength in her neck went next. She hung her head with tired eyes, leaving her to stare down at the pool of blood forming like a shadow at the base of the tree.

She closed her eyes, wheezing slowly as she was losing her fight to stay alive. Somewhere in the night, there were voices continuing on as if nothing had happened.

* * *

Coura found herself floating amid a gray space, staring up at the nothingness above. There was no ground in this place, or clouds, or … anything. Somehow she knew that as she closed her eyes in contentment there was also no pain here. Her mind was at rest too, though she could not remember what had happened to bring her here.

After a moment, she felt another presence. Her body twisted around to a sitting position, still floating in space, to see a shadow standing at eye level with her.

"So, you are finally here," the feminine voice said with amusement.

"Where are we?" Coura asked as she glanced around, unafraid.

"This is your *chi-alve.*"

"Chi-alve?"

The shadow nodded. "Yes, or your 'soul space.' All creatures have one. It is the center of your being where your conscious resides, but you should only be here through a meditation of sorts."

"Why am I here?" she asked, fear starting to penetrate her peacefulness.

Although the shadow had no face, Coura could sense its disapproval. "Because you are weak. You allowed yourself to lose, thus sacrificing your body and forcing your spirit here as a last resort. Most mortals experience this before they die."

"I'm going to die?"

"No," the shadow's head shook, "not as long as you allow me to save you."

At the mention of death, Coura wanted to be rescued so bad her chest ached, yet she wondered who this other person in *her* soul space was. "Who are you?"

"I cannot tell you now, not here. However, time is running out for you to decide. Will you die here or let me bring your body back from destruction?"

* * *

If Will had been afraid before, he was now petrified by what he saw the stranger do. He had known Coura didn't stand a chance against an angel's speed and strength, yet he let her fight. *I should have told them about Byron. I should have tried to run. At least I would be doing something other than sit here uselessly!*

Tears streamed down his cheeks through eyes glued to Coura's limp body hanging from the tree trunk. Somewhere in the recesses of his still sane mind he was thankful it was too dark for him to see her in detail or else he would have vomited.

"It really is a shame she didn't have very much stamina," the female angel said as she walked over to rejoin them. "Not very many humans can hold their own for very long. I was beginning to think she would be more entertaining."

"Pity humans aren't made of tougher stuff," the man said with disappointment.

"Shut *up!*"

They both turned to stare down at Will. "Oh, now he talks!"

"I said *shut up!*" Will squeezed his eyes closed, unable to bear their presence. He wanted to scream and cry and run to Coura's side. The hiss of a sword being drawn had his eyes shooting open and darting to the male. A moment later the silver tip was at Will's throat. He stared wide-eyed and hopeless at the angel who had lost all hint of amusement.

"Now then, enough of that. It's going to be dawn in a couple of hours so I would rather not drag this out. If you don't tell us where the mage is, you shall share the same fate as her. Actually, it will probably be worse since I like to keep my playthings *alive* much longer than Elsa."

Will swallowed though his mouth was dry. No sound came from it as his lips attempted to form words. He prayed again but knew death was coming. For deep down, beneath the fear, weakness, and pain was a commitment to Byron. Will would not sacrifice his freedom for Byron's life, not for the life of anyone dear to him. *Anyone except Coura...*

He looked up into the man's face, hoping to convey his resolve. It must have worked, for the angel was at first confused, then understanding. "So be it," he mumbled and began to raise his sword.

A sort of contentment fell over Will at that moment, as if accepting his fate brought satisfaction in death. He closed his eyes and prayed one last time for his death to not be in vain. Seconds ticked by, drawing out what Will expected to be a brief execution. However, when he opened his eyes, he saw both of the angels' attention fixed elsewhere. They were watching the tree where Coura hung from the trunk with narrowed eyes. Suddenly, the female charged it with fists illuminated by lightning that sparked around them.

"Elsa, wait!" The male reached out for her, caught off guard by the unexpected action.

In the dark, Will couldn't tell what they saw or understand what they felt. In the next moment, with the lightning brightening up part of the area, his jaw dropped. Coura's hands were not only on the blade, but it was nearly out of her chest. *There's no way! She has already lost so much blood, though. How could she have survived something like that, let alone have the strength to keep going?*

With a sickening gush, the sword came free. Coura fell and managed to land on her feet somehow. Will gasped as she did but was shocked to find the air so humid he barely felt like he breathed in any air at all.

What's happening? It's the middle of the night, but the air is so heavy. Unless... unless this is magic. Could it be caused by the angel's lightning? Somehow Will doubted that, which made him grow anxious. At the moment, he was more concerned with the woman charging Coura, lightning as ready as any weapon and poised to strike.

He tried calling out, telling her to run, but his voice broke on her name. The shout was lost by the crackling bolts anyway. Will was left to watch as the angel reached his friend and threw her spell.

What none of them had seen or were expecting was Coura's magic. The angel's lightning struck something like a wall of glittering, dark glass, making a sound like metal scraping metal. Will immediately covered his ears and watched as Elsa was pushed back by the sheer blockage of her magic. She lost control of the rest of her lightning then, sending sparks and bolts shooting around the area. Thankfully, none came close to her companion or Will, but one bolt struck the trunk of a nearby tree. It split in half and caught on fire immediately. Within a scary amount of time, the fallen branches transferred their flames to two other trees, illuminating their space with an eerie red-and-orange glow.

I have to get out of here! This may be my only chance, Will thought with panic as smoke rose around them. Still, he did not want to leave Coura. Without a glance at the others, he turned around and ran as fast as he could into the trees behind them. Once out of the open, he ducked behind the trunk of the nearest tree and looked back. From here, he could see the entire area fine but wasn't in the way and could easily hide or run.

The shield in front of Coura dispersed, and he noticed a shadow behind her back solidifying in the dim light. *Those kind of look like... wings?* He squinted against the still-rising smoke to make her figure out better as she stepped forward. Will's heart stopped as there was no doubt remaining. They were definitely wings along her back, except they were colored black as a moonless night. Unlike the angels' wings, which appeared soft to touch, the feathers on these prickled with what he could only think to be disdain.

The female angel yelled something as she approached again to unleash another blast of lightning. It reached Coura, but she sidestepped it just as the bolt would have struck her, blowing up the tree behind her instead. Three more times Elsa fired her spells. Each time, Coura dodged them with ease and came closer. It was when the angel was retracing her steps toward her companion that Will caught something shining in the firelight. Somehow, Coura was still holding on to the other's blade, covered with her own blood.

"Who are you?" the male angel yelled out of nowhere, causing Will to jump. He was trying to draw Coura's attention, but she was fixated on his companion. He shouted again and received the same lack of response, then at last drew his own sword. As it was halfway out of its scabbard, Coura struck.

Elsa glanced back at her companion in alarm for a second. When she faced forward, Coura leapt into the air, wings spread like an aviary predator, and pounced with new speed. The angel's hands rose too late to do much but attempt to block her blade, except Coura did not use the blade first. With her empty left hand, she grabbed Elsa's hands and pulled them downward before the angel knew what she was doing. Only then did Coura bring the blade up to Elsa's throat and slice, cutting off the female angel's scream.

Will had to look away and force himself to breathe so as to not vomit at the sight of the blonde head rolling on the ground. He forced himself to continue watching sooner than he would have liked in order to catch everything that was happening.

The remaining angel, Devan, cried out his companion's name, mourning the loss of what Will believed to be a deeply personal relationship. Coura turned to face him, and indirectly Will, as if the angel's death meant nothing. Although everything about her appeared the same, her presence frightened him. The unnatural wings loomed over the rest of her body menacingly, and her clothes were ripped in multiple places with only red underneath.

Her dark, unbound hair waved gently in the slight wind moving the smoke away, and the blue eyes that he thought were always bright and full of life were quite the opposite. As she stared at her final opponent, Will realized he was afraid.

He had never in all his life heard of a creature with angel wings not colored in white. Coura's were the same size and shape as Devan's, but their demeanor was the opposite. Instead of the peaceful, divine nature the stories described, which was what Will thought when he first saw the two angels, despite their intentions, the black wings and Coura's appearance were wicked, wrong, and wholly evil in his eyes. A shiver crept down Will's spine that didn't seem to end.

A demon... That is the opposite of an angel. She's been possessed by a demon. Is she even human anymore? What happens to a person when they become possessed? Will knew very little about demons' work, as it was not a very popular topic of conversation for good reason. In fact, in most towns he briefly passed through, bringing up demons was either punishable or said to bring curses upon your descendants. He wondered if the angel was thinking the same thing as he stood unmoving while Coura walked over, sword hanging at her side to let the fresh blood soak the ground.

They faced each other as still as statues. He wondered how the angel would strike, what he would, or *could*, do to Coura. Devan's fingers curled and relaxed on the hilt, the only sign he didn't turned to stone. It was then Will understood what was actually happening. The angel wasn't thinking of how to attack. He was looking for the best escape route.

As quick as lightning, Devan leapt straight up into the air, pumped his wings to gain some height, then tightened them against his back. Coura followed a hair's breadth after but angled herself to meet him in the sky. Her sword swung for his neck, and he brought up his own blade to block with one hand while shooting a ball of fire down at her with the other. It hit square in the stomach, but Will didn't think she even noticed. One swing followed another, then another. Their swords clinked as they battled in the gray sky. She was keeping Devan's focus on defending himself to avoid letting him fly away. Will didn't see him prepare the next fireball. It just appeared suddenly to strike Coura right in the face. He heard her hiss as she pulled her head away, which gave Devan just enough time to climb higher into the air.

Coura's head shot straight up at him, and she grabbed his foot, striking as quick as a snake. In panic, Devan beat his wings harder as if to free his leg, but it was already futile. With another swing of her sword, Coura cut his foot off from the ankle and threw it into the woods. The angel howled in pain but was smart enough not to let it stop him from escaping. Faster than Will would have thought, Devan launched himself into the sky and soon disappeared past the treetop. He half expected Coura to follow. Instead, she remained suspended in the air, the black wings pumping to hold her up, and looked after Devan as he flew away.

11

Will wondered what he should do. A minute passed by, then two, and still Coura watched the sky. He hadn't noticed how tense he was until his fingers cramped from grasping the tree trunk. As quietly as he could, he pried himself away from the tree and took a couple of steps backward. He froze again and watched Coura descend to the ground. As soon as her feet touched the grass, the wings dispersed into fragments that shimmered in the firelight before fading away. Her body collapsed to the ground, where she remained unmoving.

What do I do? Will thought weakly. He waited for her to get up, for the wings to form again, or something. *Perhaps she's really dead this time.*

Although tears threatened to rise again, he was too tired to even think about breaking down. His mind was numb, and the aching in his face had returned. *I ... have to get back...*

It took him a while, especially with the smoke from the now-dying flames, but Will managed to figure out which direction Fester was in from the approaching sunrise still at least an hour away. Every step was a burden. His chest hurt from his frantic heartbeats, but once he was far enough not to see any of the firelight, he was able to breathe a little easier. The air returned to normal, and he even heard insects hesitantly chirping.

After what seemed like an eternity, Will pushed back a last branch to reveal their camp, complete with Byron and Marcus snoring away as if nothing had happened. He took a seat with his back against his still-rolled sleeping bag and remained that way until dawn finally approached.

* * *

Byron covered his eyes as sunlight threatened to blind him, then remained motionless until his thirst finally got the better of him. With a groan, he pushed himself up, then took a long pause to settle his stomach. His head hurt worse, but the stomach pain was a close second. With a mind too muddled to process anything, Byron naturally started looking for water. He fumbled around for far too much time through bags until he finally grabbed their water skin and chugged every last drop. In the morning fog, he heard snoring and saw Marcus next to him. That was all he could take in before passing out again on his bedroll.

Later in the day, he woke up feeling a little more alive as getting up was easier on his head and stomach. He relieved himself in the woods, drank more water, and located the bag of food. The thought of most of the fruit and cheeses made his stomach turn, but he found plain bread and nibbled on it.

What happened last night? It hurt, but he remembered spending the day at the tavern and getting drunk with Cintra. They caught up on each other's lives before she found another bottle of that sweet wine. *Leave it to her to get me like this. I haven't been drunk in months.*

With something in his stomach, Byron was able to function better. He winced as he glanced up at the sky to see it was early afternoon. *Great. I slept through most of the day. Well, it looks like we will have to head out today then. Wait a minute... What are we doing in the woods? What happened to the inn?*

His eyes darted around the trees and their camp. His head spun in protest, and he cursed himself for looking around so

162

fast. Will was sitting against his bedroll, facing the forest, while Marcus was still sleeping.

"Will?"

The boy didn't move, so Byron assumed he was sleeping as well. Coura wasn't in the area, but he knew she couldn't stand sitting around waiting for them to wake up. He made a note to mentally prepare himself for a lecture from her when she returned. With his foot, Byron nudged the soldier across from him. Marcus groaned and cracked open one eye.

"It's time for us to get going," Byron told him as he got to his feet.

Very slowly, the soldier stretched and got up to relieve himself elsewhere, stumbling as he did so. *I see I'm not the only one who enjoyed Fester,* he thought with a smile.

Overall, it was a pleasant visit and an enjoyable break from their journey. However, as he wandered around the area for water, he remembered their goal and told himself today they would focus on getting back to the MAA promptly. There was a stream a lot farther out than he liked, but Byron took his time washing away his drunkenness and drinking his fill before returning.

"There's a stream a good distance that way," he said to Marcus as he entered the camp.

"Good. I feel terrible," the boy said rubbing his head. As he passed by, Byron noticed dried blood on the side of his head.

"What happened?"

"Huh?"

"Your head," Byron pointed to his temple. "You've got a good-sized cut there."

"I'm not sure. I have to clean up," was all Marcus said before disappearing into the woods.

He spotted Will in the same spot and came over. "You up yet?"

He put a hand on the boy's shoulder and was startled to see him jump. Byron knelt beside Will, who was watching the woods with red eyes. Very slightly, the boy was trembling. "Will, what happened to you? Talk to me."

He shook Will's shoulders gently until he came to, blinking several times before peeling his eyes away from the trees. "Byron? You're awake?"

"Yes, I'm managing. What's wrong? You look like you haven't slept a wink."

"I couldn't... not when... she's... there..." He trailed off into mumbles and watched the woods again.

"Who's there? What are you talking about?" It was then that Byron noticed how bruised the boy's face was, and that he smelled faintly of smoke. "Tell me about last night," he ordered, deciding to start over.

Perhaps this is why we are outside of Fester. If something happened at the tavern, or even at the inn, we might have to go back. That other presence was chasing us, but I can't sense it anymore. Could it have something to do with this?

"I spent the day like you said," Will began in a whisper. "When I got back, we ... we went ... to get you..."

"You and Coura?"

The boy nodded, but something about the memory sprang upon him. In a split second, he crumbled into a mess of tears, head in his hands, shaking with sobs.

Now Byron was concerned. "Will, I need you to tell me what happened."

Will only shook his head, his whole body wavering. "I-I-I t-t-tried to k-keep them aw-way," he stammered.

"Who? Keep who away?"

"Then C-C-Coura came..." More sobbing.

"What's going on?" Marcus asked as he returned from the other end of their camp.

"We need to leave," Byron said shortly.

"Why?" Byron cast Marcus a look as if to say "something's wrong," which the assistant general read immediately. "I'll pack everything up."

With Marcus taking care of the camp, Byron focused his attention on putting Will together. "Where's Coura?" he asked in a low voice. Whatever was going on, he needed to make sure she wasn't the cause.

After another minute, Will seemed to have cried himself out for the moment and was able to talk without breaking down.

"Where is Coura?" Byron asked again.

With a shaky hand, Will pointed into the woods. "I ... she's still..."

"All right, let's go for a walk then," Byron said, helping the boy to his feet. "We'll be back," he told Marcus, who nodded.

Over the years, Byron's ventures had brought him face-to-face with people who had suffered through traumatic experiences. Fires, raiders, sickness, and more all caused ordinary towns-folk to react in unpredictable ways. Some lost all personality and closed themselves away. Others were frantic with anger or sadness, worse than Will's breakdown. Most recovered with attention and comfort and were able to accept what had happened and move on. The memories still hurt and haunted them, but only time can heal unseen scars. There was a small percentage of people Byron worked with who had suppressed their past experiences in order to work toward a brighter future.

Coura was one example. When Byron brought her back to the academy, she remembered only fragments of what had happened to her home village. It was nothing helpful to him. When the messengers reported the town destroyed and abandoned, it was a relief that Coura was OK. There was some hurt, but within a few weeks, the details were forgotten, which Byron thought was for the best. She also showed no interest in her past life, and that spared him from telling her when the townsfolk returned weeks later and what his messenger had reported.

In Will's case, as they walked and talked, the boy came back to life, recalling some pieces from the previous night. Byron put together that the guards were looking to arrest him, so Will and Coura had moved them all out into the woods for safety. It seemed harmless, so why couldn't Will continue past that?

He's stumbling on words, will barely mention names, and goes silent whenever he tries to tell me more. Now I can smell smoke, and we must be quite a distance from Fester.

Not long after, Will stopped and started his tale over again for about the tenth time, then the boy paused and very slowly pushed back a thin branch. Beyond, Byron could see a clearing where smoke was rising from fallen trees.

"Is there danger?" he asked Will in a low voice, his body tense and preparing for the worst.

"I ... don't think so. I don't know."

"Wait here," he whispered, then proceeded to creep through the brush. Try as he might, Byron couldn't keep from making quite a lot of noise. With each crunch of a twig or swish of leaves, he cursed himself for letting his hangover affect his body so much. Once he could make out the entire clearing, Byron froze. There were no creatures or people in sight, but he could make out a lot of blood and charred earth. *There was fighting here last night,* he thought with a sinking feeling.

166

As his eyes glanced over the fire, blood, and broken trees, he saw a body on the ground at the other end. He recognized it as Coura, and she wasn't moving.

Although he wanted to run straight to her, Byron knew better than to burst out into the open. Carefully, he emerged and held himself to a walking pace. Once he knew there were no traps or an ambush, he sprinted over and knelt beside his student. He turned her over onto her back and nearly wept at the tears in her shirt and blood covering her body. Gently, he shook her shoulders.

"Come on, Coura!"

Nothing happened. He put an ear to her chest. This time, he did let out a cry of relief, and tears stung his eyes as he heard her breathing. "Will," Byron called to the boy, who now watched from the edge of the clearing, "I need your help. She's breathing, but I can't see any injuries like this."

"She's dead," Will said just loud enough for him to hear.

"No, she's not. We have to hurry or else..." He glanced up to Will in surprise and saw his eyes elsewhere. Following his gaze, Byron was stunned to see the body of another woman. Her head was mere feet away. Finally, it clicked.

He was here last night. He watched *the woman die and Coura get hurt. The boy is in shock!* He looked between Coura and Will twice before deciding he wouldn't get anywhere without Will. He set Coura down lightly before grabbing Will's arm and pulling him into the trees.

"It's OK," he said when they were outside of viewing distance. Without another word, Byron pulled Will into his arms. That seemed to be the boy's cue to snap, for he broke down again. Byron held him close, only moving when the boy threatened to vomit, and looking away politely as he did throw up in a bush nearby.

Byron had seen death in many forms over the years. Decapitation was one of the worst and most uncommon that had given him nightmares. Once Will was finished, he walked back and stared at the ground, holding his stomach.

"I'm all right now," he said quietly. Byron saw he was still shaking, but this time with a sort of ease.

"I know it's hard for you, Will," he began in the softest voice possible, "but I need you to help me. Do you think you can find a stream or pool of water?" The boy nodded and turned to look farther.

That's one problem solved for now. Byron hurried back to the clearing. Coura was still unconscious, but he wouldn't be able to do much without washing some of the blood away. However, before going to her to try and stop the bleeding, he needed to take care of two other things. First, he moved the woman's body behind one of the trees and out of sight. He noticed she had a shirt with two slits in the back but no blood there besides what came from her split neck. He tried not to look at her face as he reunited the head with the body, but Byron couldn't help but notice the expression of fear stuck on it.

Next, he tapped into his dark magic and cast a small ice storm spell to put out the rest of the flames. Somehow, they had managed to be contained to a handful of trees, but it was better for him to be safe.

Will returned then, appearing more alive than he had been all day. "I found a stream close by." Byron noticed his eyes wandering over to where the woman's body had been, and the boy showed some relief that it was gone.

"Good. Now let's get going." He checked Coura's breathing once more, noting how normal it was, as if she were only sleeping. "All right, she should be fine." He lifted her up in his arms carefully. She was extremely light and very pale.

It didn't take them more than a few minutes to reach the fairly wide stream, which was more of a small river, that Will had picked out. As the boy watched from the bank, Byron climbed into the water up to his waist and gently lowered Coura's body in. The stream carried away the blood, turning the water a reddish purple. He began softly rubbing her chest as modestly as he could. From the amount of blood, that was most likely where her main wound was; however, Byron was confused to see only unmarred skin underneath her shirt. As a precaution, he tore it off, which wasn't difficult considering how it was shredded to pieces. There wasn't a scratch on her torso. Byron gently wiped her arms and legs but also found them clean besides the blood.

Once her body was rinsed, he brought her back up to the shore. Will blushed at her bare chest and turned away quickly when they approached. Byron set her down in the grass, removed his own shirt, and put it on her. It was far too big, but that hardly mattered now. He watched her continue breathing, puzzled by their situation.

"Is she going to be OK?" Will asked, still facing away.

"I think so, but we won't know until she wakes up. Her body is fine, but I wonder if there are internal injuries."

"What!" Will spun around and knelt beside Byron. His hands went straight to the center of her chest. He did the same analysis as Byron, but with more disbelief. "That's impossible!"

"What's wrong?"

"How can she be unhurt?"

"Perhaps that was not her blood." Byron considered whether she had expended her energies, causing her body to shut down momentarily to recover. She had never done that before, and it would make sense since this was her first time in a fight away from home.

Will only shook his head. "No, no, no, I saw it all. She was stabbed right here!" He pointed to the center of her chest again.

Byron raised his eyebrows. "I think it's about time you tell me what happened after you two dragged us out of Fester."

Will began with what Byron had already picked up on. He and Coura met in their room at sundown as they had been instructed to do. When neither he nor Marcus returned, they left to find them but discovered the guards searching for their group to arrest Byron and possibly frame him for desertion. That part didn't surprise Byron as much as the thought of Marcus's comrades going behind their superior's back by disobeying his order to stand down. Will found Coura taking Marcus out of the tavern, and they decided to camp in the woods. While Will made three trips to the inn to pack and retrieve their belongings, Coura went to the tavern to get Byron. The muddled memories came slowly back as he remembered being hauled from Cintra's room.

"When I had the last of the bags, I thought it was too late for Coura to be out looking for you. As I was heading for the tavern, a woman approached me in the clearing. She asked me to help her find a friend who had run off into the woods. I've been warned about such temptresses robbing a man blind by luring him away from the roads and knocking him over the head, so I refused. When I tried to run, she grabbed my arm, covered my mouth, and forced me into the forest with inhuman strength. Thankfully, I at least knew where we were, though she didn't figure out you two and our things were in the camp nearby. I was dragged to that clearing where the woman and a man she called Devan asked me about you."

Byron remained silent during Will's explanation, intent on capturing every word. The boy looked up at him then with red-rimmed eyes. "I didn't tell them anything, I promise! They hit me in the face a couple times and threatened to burn me, but I kept quiet!"

The pleading on Will's face warmed Byron's heart. "I believe you, Will," he said with a small smile. "I also know it wasn't fair for you to be in that situation, but it means a lot that you stood up for me."

The boy's cheeks began turning pink as he continued. "I knew I had to, is all. Anyway, they threatened to burn my face when Coura came out of the trees and told them to stop." Will paused.

"What is it?" Byron pressed.

"I didn't mention it, but ... the man and woman, they were angels, Byron."

"Angels?" he repeated in disbelief. "Are you sure?"

"I've never been more sure in my life! They tried sweet-talking me too, saying they were my friends, and a friend of Verona would not deny their request."

"I've never thought an angel would threaten someone before," Byron interrupted.

"My thoughts exactly. You should have seen their wings, though. Their feathers looked soft and magical."

"Did the woman have them when she first found you?"

Will shook his head. "No, it wasn't until we were alone. They seemed to cast them, like they did with the fire."

Byron noted this to himself. *It's been a while since anyone has seen an angel. I don't ever recall them manifesting wings like I do a spell...* His thoughts were cut short as Will went on.

He told Byron of Coura's attempt to save him and how the woman pinned her to a tree with her sword. What scared Byron the most were Will's descriptions, true to detail. The boy was very brave for not only surviving such an encounter but also for forcing himself to memorize and recall such information.

"So that's why you say it's odd she has no wound," Byron repeated quietly.

"Yes. I was sure she had bled to death, but somehow she pulled the sword out of herself and..." A haunted look came over his face as his eyes fell on Coura. "Byron, she had them too."

"Had what?"

"Wings. I wasn't sure at first, but when she came closer, they were like the angels' except they were black." Byron was speechless but didn't dare interrupt this time.

"I've never seen or heard of anything like it! Her eyes were different too, like she was someone else. She sprang off the tree, dodged the woman's lightning bolts, and cut off her head. Then she almost stopped the other from escaping by slicing off his foot in the air. When he got away, Coura watched him fly off before falling to the ground, and her wings disappeared. That's when I left," Will concluded, looking pretty pale.

Byron asked him about specific details, such as her appearance and behavior, but he didn't know where to begin processing this story. *Firstly, he mentioned the angels could manifest wings without effort out of thin air. Then, they can cast spells like lightning and fire. Only highly trained light mages are able to manipulate their energies into that form, which is rare since I thought it required knowledge of dark magic.*

He cast a look of concern at his unconscious student. *Oh, Coura, I don't know what to do with you. I never heard of someone possessing wings besides the angels, let alone wings of a different color. What Will described sounds close to demonic possession, but not many who see or experience it live to explain. None have ever had wings before. I guess we'll have to wait for you to wake up to tell us.*

Her body remained still except for her chest, which rose slightly to show she was breathing. Normally anyone having anything to do with demons was cast away or executed, even if it wasn't on purpose. Most cities and towns did not tolerate any sort of demonic energies, which was good since it only brought on unforetold troubles.

"Will," Byron said at last, "let's head back to the camp."

"But, what should we do about—"

"Speak of this to no one," he warned, rising and taking Coura in his arms.

"You're bringing her back? Aren't you worried about what could happen with a demon in your home?"

Byron faced Will without attempting to hide his surprise. It made him defensive, and he wanted to lash out at such hateful behavior. *How quickly he turned on Coura after mentioning demons, but how can I blame him after all he's been through? Besides, I wasn't there to confirm demonic energy. I have only his word to go on for now until she wakes up.*

"Listen to me," Byron said more firmly than he had ever spoken to Will, "We have to leave this place and head back to the academy as soon as possible. If one of those angels flew away, there's no doubt they will be back. Not only for me, but for all of us. I won't condemn Coura until I can test her for demonic energy when she wakes up."

"But, she—"

"Enough," Byron interrupted, letting his headache from too much thinking on a hangover show. Will winced and shied away.

"I understand what you're feeling," Byron followed in a softer tone. "You were willing to sacrifice your life to keep us safe, and I thank you immensely for that. Please, I'm begging you, do *not* mention this to anyone for now, not even Marcus. There's something else going on here. I don't want word spreading about angels and demon possessions until I can discuss it with the other master mages at the MAA. I promise I won't let anything like that happen again."

Will did not answer but appeared satisfied, so Byron began heading for their camp, letting the boy put together his own opinions as they hurried back in silence.

12

At the camp Marcus had everything packed and ready to go. He even went out of his way to make them all meager sandwiches from the leftovers. As soon as he saw Coura hanging from Byron's arms, he was on his feet asking the same questions Byron had been asking Will earlier.

As he set his student down, ate his sandwich quickly, and shouldered his pack, Byron briefly explained how Coura and Will moved them into the woods and why. He expected Marcus to be upset at their distrust of the soldiers, but he only shook his head.

"I can't believe they would go behind my back like that," he mumbled awkwardly.

"I'm sure they were concerned about punishment for disobedience by whoever gave them those orders," Byron said as he again took Coura in his arms and led them out of their camp in search of the road leading to East Hoover.

"Perhaps, but I don't know who could have given them orders that override mine."

He means that someone outranking him wants me arrested and for him to take over delivery of the documents. I wish I could trust him, but it's still better to keep things simple for now.

"So then, what happened to Coura and Will?" Marcus continued in a hushed tone. Will strayed behind just far enough to give them some privacy.

"The mage who was following us all this time made an appearance. Will accidentally ran into it in the woods and was trapped in a clearing north of our camp. Coura went to rescue him and drained herself protecting him."

Marcus gave Byron a confused look. "What do you mean she 'drained' herself?"

"It's fairly common for young mages who aren't experienced in magical combat to use up all of their energies. Actually, you can compare it to physically fighting. When you work your muscles too hard and for too long, your body shuts down to recover afterward. From my experience with drainings, she should be waking up within a day or two and will be famished."

The assistant general nodded at the comparison and was silent for a while as they found the main road. With his help, Byron shifted Coura onto his back as if she were a sleeping child to appear more natural. There was a surprising amount of people heading in and out of Fester, most with a wagon or cart pulled by some beast. It was easy for them to sneak out under their cover.

Once outside of the city, the main road broke off into three paths heading west to Verona, north to East Hoover, and east to some smaller towns and ultimately the coastal cities. Most of their temporary companions took one of the other two paths heading west or east. By then, the sun was setting, and the three were forced to create a makeshift camp along the side of the road.

While Marcus and Will showed disagreement with his decision to stop, Byron assured them the other presence was gone, thanks to Coura, which was partly true. They rose before sunrise, all except Coura, and began the last leg of their journey in a tired silence. Marcus offered to carry Coura piggyback, for which Byron and his sore back were grateful.

"We've got about another couple of hours before we reach East Hoover," Byron told them in reassurance as the road forked for a final time. They were the only people heading in that direction.

"That's good news," Marcus said with a sigh.

Even Will felt well enough to talk after that, and Byron brought up a helpful observation as they took a break along the road. He knew this trail better than anyone, given how often he had traveled it. "Just past these ferns along the trail is a wild orchard. I usually stop here to pick a few apples to carry me the rest of the way. Why don't we head there for a bit to refresh ourselves?"

The boys eagerly agreed, with rumbling stomachs, and hurried to the space containing about a dozen different apple trees now in season. Marcus leaned Coura up against one of the trees in plain sight and went climbing for the fruit nearest the top. Will hesitantly followed, while Byron was able to reach up and pick the few he desired.

"Hey, I see something else," Will called out from above. He rushed down the tree as Byron hurried over in case he slipped. After descending, the boy ran over to the edge of the orchard to a bush.

"Look, gooseberries!" The green, round fruits were just ripe enough to eat, and Will began harvesting them eagerly, careful not to prick himself on their thorns.

"That's odd. I don't remember this bush," Byron said as he picked a few and savored their tartness.

After they had helped themselves, he ordered the boys to fill the empty food pack with some of the fruit before they left. This would not only keep them going, but Byron always tried to keep some fresh fruit in his room. They didn't need to know that, though.

He took a deep breath, enjoying the warm day, then started at a groan from where his student rested behind him. "Coura!" He spun around and went to her as she began to sit up.

"Byron?" She held her head with one hand and rubbed her eyes with the other. "Where are we?" she grumbled in a harsh voice.

"How do you feel?" he asked her instead.

"I don't... I asked you first," Coura retorted weakly.

Just like her old self, he thought, relaxing a trifle.

"We left Fester yesterday afternoon and are a little ways outside of East Hoover. We should be back home in a couple of hours."

"We're that close already? Wait, we've been on the road for a day?"

"Take it easy, you're still weak."

"Weak? What did I...?" Her voice trailed off as she looked at the ground in thought. Suddenly, her eyes widened a little as if she had just recalled something and her hand moved quickly to her chest. It rested on the exact spot Will had pointed out yesterday.

"What is it?" he pushed with feigned curiosity.

She glanced around with more alertness. "It's nothing. Where is Will?"

"He's fine, but we need to get going now." He helped her to her feet as Marcus and Will returned.

"Coura, you're all right," the first exclaimed with sincerity.

"How's your head?" she asked in an unamused voice.

"I don't know what happened, but I take it you do?"

She just smiled and dug into the apples they had stored with fervor. Once she finished eating her fill, they made their way back to the road.

* * *

Coura tried her best to hide her confusion, but had to bite her tongue to avoid snapping at Byron for the continuous questioning. She was both tired and frustrated and did not want to say anything about what had happened two nights ago until she could put it together herself. What was worse were her companions' behavior.

Only two hours away and then I can find some alone time, she told herself patiently. At the moment, she wanted to make sure Will was all right and figure out what had happened with the angels after she had been stabbed.

I know it wasn't a dream. Will was there with two angels. I remember the slice in my arm, and I remember being stabbed through the chest, but there are no wounds. No one mentioned that we stopped in town, so how could it have healed without a light mage? The angels didn't heal me, but they didn't kill me either. I can't sense their presence at all, so what happened? This doesn't make sense! Coura racked her brain to no avail, remembering nothing after the female angel's fight with her.

Byron wouldn't leave her alone or let her talk to Will, who avoided looking her in the eyes and trailed far behind. At first, Marcus doted over her as if she couldn't handle herself. He offered her a shoulder to lean on, then a hand when her legs were still stiff, but she shooed him away. Finally, he followed behind with Will, and the two talked while casting glances at her from time to time. Meanwhile, Byron asked her to tell him what had taken place two nights ago. She made sure to go into as much detail about everything, especially Byron's drunkenness, about which he didn't approve.

Only an hour or so away now.

"All right, I know I misbehaved! You haven't told me what took place *after* you brought us into the woods."

She knit her brows in frustration. "I did. I said I don't remember."

"Coura," he began in a tone she knew all too well. Byron often used it when she had misbehaved in classes, which meant he was about to lecture her on poor attitudes, respect for elders, or some other life lesson.

She cut him off before he could go further with a wave of her hand that made her head throb. "Byron, I told you what I know twice now. I'm done talking to you!"

"We're not finished," he threatened, then lightened up slightly. "Will told me more."

"Then go talk to him," she growled in reply.

Byron decided he had pushed her enough for now and backed off. Coura could not bear walking beside him and picked up her pace to put herself a few feet at the front, against the protest of her legs.

Did Will send the angels away or convince them to heal me? Byron doesn't know, so he couldn't have made it in time to help, so who chased them off? Who healed me? What does Will know that I can't recall?

* * *

Seeing the academy in the distance was a relief to everyone, especially Byron. He had just about lost his patience with Coura's stubborn behavior, which only grew worse after she had distanced herself from him. Will didn't seem pleased she was awake, though Marcus was. Byron figured he wasn't used to helping rescue a lady in distress and took pleasure in being seen as chivalrous. He wanted to assure Marcus that the feeling fades fast after actually *doing* something to save someone, but he would let the boy figure it out on his own.

They made great time getting to East Hoover, but Byron's next few hours would now consist of reporting on Verona, the final decisions discussed at the palace, and somehow bringing up Coura and the angels in the midst of their frustration. *This isn't going to be easy, for me or Symon. The discussion will set the pace for a rough future, but first I've got to take care of these three.*

"All of you, gather around," he stopped in the road and waited for them to huddle near him. "Once we enter the academy, Will and Marcus, I would like you to come with me to the headmaster's office. We will find you a room, Marcus, and then you're free to relax. I can even arrange for a tour if you are interested."

The boy nodded sharply. "Actually, I've been directed to observe your delivery of the documents and add any additional pieces of information."

Byron avoided groaning out loud with annoyance as Marcus spoke without hesitation. *Sometimes I forget he is another soldier under King Hernan's thumb. I wish this could be easier, and I was starting to like him.*

"Fine, but that won't be until tomorrow at the soonest. I need to take care of Will first, and the headmaster will have to arrange the other master mages to meet. I'll make sure you're told when that is."

It hurt Byron to see the trust in Marcus's eyes at his lie. In actuality, he would need the assistant general out of the way when he saw Symon so he could tell him everything first in private. In turn, Symon would brief the other instructors so they would be able to prepare themselves for the final discussion. Even then he wasn't sure they would allow anyone else into that meeting.

"Now, Will, we're going straight to find you some space as well and vouch for what we discussed." The other boy nodded with a smile. Byron knew this part would be simple, so he was happy to follow through.

Finally, he glanced at Coura, who dug the toe of her boot into the dirt in a casual manner. "What are you going to do, Coura?" He chose to ask her instead of ordering her to stay somewhere alone and out of the way because he figured he would get the same response, only it would be *her* choice, not *his* order.

"I'm going to my room to unpack and probably find something to eat," she said shortly, and Byron smiled to himself.

"OK, let's get going then."

* * *

For the next five days, Coura tried her best to stay out of everyone's way while the academy went wild with the news Byron had brought. King Hernan had issued a law stating that once a student from the academy turned sixteen, they were to be transferred to Verona for additional training for three years. There, they would act as mage-soldiers in Asteom's army and obey whatever orders their supervisors gave, including being stationed around the country if necessary. In addition to defending the capital, should the country go to war, they would fight on the battlefield. After serving their time, the students would graduate and have the option to stay in the army or to be assigned as guards somewhere most suited to them around the country.

Byron hadn't mentioned anything to Coura during their travels. Not that she minded, but he had been very secretive for months before. Either someone seriously screwed up by letting the information slip outside of the meetings, or it was purposely mentioned to prepare the older trainees. With how the instructors responded, she figured it was the former.

Classes had been canceled and students were advised not to leave the academy until things were settled. However, being cooped up seemed to make the building tense. Her classmates whispered under their breaths around her at lunch. Almost all were fearful of the idea of being stationed for three years somewhere they wouldn't be suited for with strangers.

"There is no way I'd let them put me on a battlefield," a younger girl named Bridgette whispered fiercely to their table. "How could they let a law like this be passed?"

"At least you got two years left until you're sixteen. Next year, I *will* be! What if there's a war with the northern country? I don't think I could stomach it," another boy named Robin whispered back. His black hair was ruffled from combing through it with his fingers all day.

"What about you, Coura? You are already sixteen, aren't you?" Bridgette now asked her in a low voice.

"We all have weapons training," Coura began in a bored tone, "and we are all suited to using magic. I doubt their generals would be stupid enough to put us in positions where we would be wasted." Coura continued eating her meal, even though she barely tasted it.

"Really?"

She nodded, swallowed the bland bite, and pushed her plate away. "Of course. They *want* more mages in their army. Why would they be so reckless? That's not considering if this law even stands for long."

The table relaxed slightly. "You sound just like Master Byron," Bridgette giggled and timidly smiled up at her.

Coura returned the smile and shrugged. "Trust me, no one here would let us be put in harm's way if they didn't feel we were ready."

That was three days ago when the trainees first began spreading the word. Now, when nothing had been accepted fully or denied, there was a lot of uncertainty and fear shadowing everyone Coura was around. It had become so predominant that she decided to eat meals in her room and focus on training alone. She hadn't seen Byron or Marcus since they had separated upon arrival. Will joined her for meals at first to warm up to her group of casual friends, but she noticed he still would not move too close or meet her eyes. This made her even more curious about what took place in the forest outside of Fester, about the pieces of her memory still missing. After a few days, he found some light mages interested in herbology, and she stopped seeing him.

Coura laid in her bed to stare up at the ceiling and wonder what would happen next. *I can't stand it here,* she realized after a minute of silence except for birds chirping nonchalantly outside of her open window. *Now that I have been out around the country, I don't think there is anything more I can learn from being here except from Byron. Maybe it is better I go back to Verona. I never seriously fought a soldier before, and who knows what I could learn from them. If only those awful noblemen and ladies weren't trouncing around and the servants didn't spy on everyone every single second, it might actually be a decent place.*

She considered returning to the sparring field for the second time that day but decided to visit one of the classrooms reserved for dark magic practice instead. However, as she sat up and walked over to close the window, someone knocked at her door. She quickly bolted the window shut and opened the door to see Marcus wearing his most professional expression.

"The headmaster, instructors, and I would like to speak with you." Her laugh echoed through the hall as she pushed past him and began making her way to the chamber reserved for important faculty meetings.

"Why are you so serious?" she turned to see him close behind.

"What do you mean?" he said just as uptight.

"Come on, Marcus. We both know each other, so you can stop the general nonsense."

"I'm only trying to represent my position as *assistant* general. This is probably the first time anyone here has seen a second-rank soldier on duty."

"OK, sure. Why do they need to see me? You didn't mention that yet."

He paused briefly, then spoke in a low voice. "It's about what happened outside of Fester."

"Oh, right." She went quiet and decided it would mean more to Marcus if he led her inside, so she slowed so he could move ahead. Shortly after, they were at the entrance to the meeting chamber.

"Please sit," he pointed to the lone chair next to the door.

"Am I not allowed inside?"

"Not yet. Will went in right before I left to get you. He's supposed to tell us what happened first since he remembers more." Marcus leaned against the opposite wall with his arms crossed. When he didn't move, she asked why he was not in the room.

"Byron asked me to stay outside," he said with some disapproval.

"Why?"

He shook his head. "I don't know, but he promised to tell me once all of it is discussed. Since it's the academy's business, I didn't argue."

"I guess that makes sense."

In the silence that followed, Coura rested her elbows on her knees and stared down at the floor. For what seemed like hours, she remained fixated on one spot, trying to remember anything that had happened after blacking out. Still, Will did not come out, and Coura and Marcus waited. The longer she sat there, the more frustrated she grew with herself for the lost memories, and at Byron for calling her here just to sit around.

Finally, Coura stood up and began storming down the hall. Marcus was caught off guard and quickly hurried after her. "Where are you going?"

"You can tell Byron I'll be in the training field whenever they need me. I won't sit around and wait forever."

"Coura, hold on!"

Outside was best since she needed to get some fresh air to cool her head. Ignoring Marcus's persistence, she chose to go to a secluded area where she and Byron usually practiced magic and weapons work. To Marcus's credit, he did not attempt to reach out to her but eventually hesitated long enough for her to turn a corner and lose him.

What is so important that they need Will for this long? What more could he remember, and why won't they let me in?

13

The training grounds made up the east and west spaces outside of the academy building. The first side was reserved for physical combat, while the other was used for magic. This way, the energies and spells could be contained, and students not working with magic weren't in danger from any potential backlash. The entire area was surrounded by a wall standing seven feet tall. Unlike the brick around the queen's garden in Verona, it was nearly impossible for someone to casually climb over the vertically placed logs.

There were a few items spread throughout the area that were necessary for their training. A well in the middle always had water, and metal bins spaced along the outer wall contained a medical kit, towels, and basic steel weapons. Although trainees couldn't use them, the instructors liked to test everyone from time to time by pretending to be an enemy. It was good practice for facing someone who wasn't a mage, and vice versa. Lastly, there were more than enough benches to rest on, as mages tended to use up a good portion of their energy in practice and during classes.

As Coura scanned the area, she was thankful there were only three other students working with one another farther off. It seemed they were practicing accuracy, as they attempted to strike a target placed on a dummy brought from inside. She continued to Byron's section of the field and took a spot at one of the benches facing the wall that overlooked the space. Only those with permission or an instructor's supervision could go into the magic grounds. Luckily, Coura not only had Byron's consent but was always able to use this space specifically set aside for his classes and private students. That was because its location was much closer to the wall than the academy since he worked with larger, more destructive spells.

With her back to the building, Coura forced herself to relax by watching the sky. There were no clouds, but many birds flitted to and fro nearly out of sight, which was enough to keep her eyes occupied while her mind worked.

What should I do? she thought regretfully. *I can't keep losing my temper like that, especially since Marcus is only doing what he was told. Maybe I am better off staying in Verona.*

The thought had crossed her mind several times over the past few days. She would be one of the first students sent to the capital if the law stood, whether she chose that path or not. *Not that I really mind leaving here or continuing my training. It's just, I feel like I don't belong in a uniform group obedient to a handful of officers. Perhaps that is my whole problem. I hate following orders from someone I don't know or trust.*

That thought made her remember Byron's lecture the night they left East Hoover. If someone like Marcus gave Coura a charge without telling her why, or it happened to be something she disagreed with, she knew in her heart it would only bring up more issues.

I suppose Marcus is all right, but I doubt I would be working with him. There's no way I could let someone boss me around and bully me into acting against my wishes. How those soldiers can stand it, I don't think I could ever understand...

Coura expected Marcus to find his way to the magic grounds and bring her back inside at any moment, yet when a hand fell on her shoulder, she still jumped slightly. "I didn't even hear you," she said with a chuckle and turned, expecting to see Marcus.

However, she was startled to see a stranger standing there with his hand resting on her shoulder instead of the assistant general. He was watching the birds above with blue eyes that mirrored the clear sky.

"I'm sorry," she apologized quickly when he said nothing. "I thought you were someone else."

"That's quite all right. A bird-watcher you are?"

Coura blinked up at the man in surprise. "No, not really." The uncomfortable silence that followed was filled by the other students' chattering, the birds crying above, and a cool breeze.

"May I join you?" the man asked suddenly.

She tilted her head at the question, uncertain why he would ask. "I suppose, but I won't be out here for long."

"That's all right. I plan on leaving shortly anyway."

He removed his hand to slip around to the front of the bench and take a seat just on the edge away from her. Now that Coura could see him better, she noted his handsome features highlighted by flowing blond hair tied into a braid at the nape of his neck. For some reason, he continued staring straight ahead or at the sky instead of at her. She had no idea what to say and decided to excuse herself to try and find Marcus.

"Are you a mage?" he asked as Coura opened her mouth to speak.

"Yes, I am. I'm a dark mage trainee."

"I see, so you don't know about light magic." Although his tone was casual, she sensed there was more beneath the man's questions.

"We study both here," she said flatly.

A flash of hurt went through his eyes before he covered it up. "Then you must know that no magic can reattach a part of the body when it is ... cut off, no matter how much energy is put into the spell."

Coura didn't answer. Something did not feel right about the man, so she began to rise and leave the stranger to himself, and probably warn someone about him once inside. As soon as she was on her feet, the man spun his head to meet her eyes. Holding them, he slowly dipped his head to glance down to his feet, leading her to do the same. Coura's eyes widened at the sight of his missing right foot, cut just above the ankle. His leg was wrapped up at the stub, and spots of red showed it still wasn't fully healed. Somehow, she knew without a doubt she was the one who had done that.

When did I... I don't remember him, but I know I did that. He looks so familiar... That's it! This man was the one with Will that night outside of Fester. He's an angel...

Seeing his stump brought back a flood of confusing memories. Coura remembered blood, a lot of blood, and the bodiless head of a woman who had died. Then, when the man tried to run, she grabbed his foot and...

Why do I recall this now? More importantly, what is he doing here? Her body froze at the thought of the same man from that night sitting mere inches away. Her eyes darted back to the man's, and she saw nothing but wild rage beneath his mask of calm. He *knew* she remembered him now. Her heart began beating frantically as her head swarmed with thoughts and memories appearing too fast for her to make any sense of them.

I have to find Byron. I have to get inside!

As soon as she moved to run to the building, he was already lunging for her. Before Coura could completely turn herself around, his fist appeared out of nowhere and connected with the side of her chest. She felt the crack of ribs as her body was knocked sideways, making her fall onto the grass next to the bench.

The pain was distracting but didn't completely block out her thoughts. She twisted with a wince to face him. Compared to the composed, handsome man she had first seen only seconds ago, this one was like a crazed animal. His eyes were wide and filled with anger while he snarled and hobbled to where she was on the ground with the help of the bench. As he did so, he hissed, "Demon child! *You* killed her and *damaged* me!"

He's insane, Coura realized as fear gripped her. *With one punch, he knocked me over. I don't stand a chance alone!*

"There you are," said a familiar voice that broke through the noise swarming around her head. Without thinking, she looked away from the man to Marcus, who was approaching from the direction of the building, and hoped to convey to him the danger with her expression alone. The angel she now remembered as Devan stopped in front of her and glanced quickly from Coura to Marcus and back.

"That's it," he growled, drawing a sword hidden by his cloak. She could only watch with horror as he raised the blade to bring it down on her.

I'm dead, she thought with dread, reciting the words over and over in her mind as the sword fell. Out of instinct, Coura raised an arm in a feeble attempt to stop the blade and closed her eyes, expecting the pain. Her eyes flung open when the sound of metal on metal rang in her ears and saw Marcus. Somehow he had predicted the attack, moved in between while drawing the sword at his waist, and blocked the angel's sword, saving her life.

"Run!" Marcus cried as he pushed the angel back.

I can't leave you, she wanted to say, but her voice was gone.

Coura wanted nothing more in that moment than to tell him everything she now remembered, about how she had murdered the woman who had nearly killed her, her inexplicable demonic powers, capturing the angel he now traded blows with and slicing off his right foot. That had to wait, for the angel, Devan, was ready to strike at her again.

Move! she yelled to herself until she was able to stand and begin running to the building, wincing at the pain in her side. Marcus continued to defend her as she did so.

As she crossed the grounds to the metal door leading inside, Coura noticed then the three other trainees who were outside working with the dummy. They were hurrying to her with concerned expressions.

"Hey, are you all right?" one called.

"What's going on?" another asked as they approached.

Coura slowed her pace and stopped. She opened her mouth to tell them to follow her inside when a voice she vaguely remembered spoke in her mind.

{*Send them inside to find help. We are not finished here.*}

She cleared her throat to voice the order. "Go inside and find the instructors in their meeting room. Tell them there's an intruder in the magical training grounds and that Coura sent you." Her stern expression and unwavering voice were all the reassurance they needed before nodding and running inside.

I have to stay outside, she thought suddenly with a strange new strength. *That angel will surely chase me, and I can't risk anyone getting hurt by something so unexpected.* Thankfully for those in the building, there were only three metal doors on this side of the academy and no windows. As long as she kept him where he was until help arrived, no one would get wrapped up in her mess.

However, as Coura watched the two men, she became worried about stopping the crazed angel. *He's moving slower because of the balance lost from his foot, but Marcus is still slower. I have to do something to keep that angel distracted.*

The clashes of their blades echoed throughout the grounds, and her first thought was to use dark magic. As she watched them dance in swordplay, though, she realized it would be near impossible to time out her spells so they wouldn't have a chance to hurt Marcus.

{*Use your sword.*}

Coura blinked with surprise at the voice in her mind. *I don't have a sword, but perhaps there is one nearby in the bins.* She spotted two metal containers, one back near the wall past Marcus and the angel, who were both holding their own, and one across the field. After a second, she decided to go for the bin farther away in the field to avoid distracting Marcus, and perhaps the angel would see her running and leave him alone.

It's my best shot. I'll have to hurry! Her lungs burned from the effort of sprinting across the area, but she was closing in on the bin. Her mind was so focused on finding a weapon that she was caught off guard at the sound of the man's cackling as she hurried on.

"It's useless," he yelled, not to Marcus, she realized, but to her.

Out of the corner of her eye, Coura caught a flash of white, then a red light followed by a cry from Marcus. She heard and glanced just in time to leap out of the way of a fireball, gasping as she landed on her bruised side. After scrambling back to her feet, she saw where the magic had hit. The angel wasn't aiming for her but for the bin, and as she approached it, she bit off a curse at the sight. His flames weren't strong enough to damage its structure, but they were hot enough to singe the metal lock shut. Coura decided against burning her hands trying to pry it open and focused her attention on the other bin nearer the fighting.

The closer she ran to the bin, the more nervous she became at being so close to their combat, which was now obviously in favor of Devan. Marcus's movements were slow and easily deflected. He was panting hard, and sweat beads covered his forehead. They both sensed her approaching, but Devan did nothing more than move toward the bin, intercepting her from getting to a weapon.

What can I do?

{*Use your sword.*}

The feminine voice spoke with some irritation this time, and Coura ignored it.

"Who are you?" Marcus yelled at the man when there was a pause in the fighting. Coura took the opportunity to inch a little closer.

"You may call me Devan, or 'Skysinger,' or whatever honorable title you deem appropriate," the angel said with wicked pride. "After all, it is only fitting that you should know the name of your killer."

"What are you doing here?" Marcus continued without hesitation.

Devan frowned and pointed his sword at Coura. "I'm here to kill the demon-child that murdered one of my sisters and took my foot."

"Coura would do no such thing," Marcus answered with a surety that startled her.

Again, the angel's hysterical laugh rang around them. "There's no reason for you to die, soldier. I suggest you spare yourself the heroics and leave."

"I will not let you run wild in this place," Marcus's voice boomed with an authority Coura hadn't heard before.

The angel's snarl replaced his crazed grin, and he glanced back and forth from Coura to Marcus, as if deciding which was worth killing first. She stood still, feeling exposed without any sort of protection. Suddenly, with a spite-filled grunt, he hurled a fireball more powerful than the first at the remaining bin to his left side. Coura's heart sank at the thought of losing her only chance at finding a weapon or armor.

"If you wish to die here, I'll oblige you," Devan growled just loud enough for them to hear.

Coura prepared to run as he cast another fireball filled with more energy than the others. Instead, she nearly cried out when he launched it at the building. With pure accuracy, it slammed into the metal door where Coura had sent the three students, and which was their nearest escape point. After his previous blasts on the bins' locks, she would have bet anything that the metal was warped enough to prevent anyone from going in, or out.

He's trapping us in here, Coura realized with shock.

"Now then, no more interruptions. I can take my time," Devan muttered. In the blink of an eye, he manifested his white wings as he did with the fire. Marcus was startled and said something to himself Coura couldn't hear before raising his sword hesitantly. Meanwhile, she recognized the angel's energy as that of the creature pursuing them outside of Fester.

Before they both could focus on the angel's new appearance and presence, Devan leapt up and launched himself forward. He struck Marcus's blade hard and continued beating down from above. While Marcus was only able to block, Coura chose to use her magic to send bolts of lightning at the sky above Devan. Her intent was not to try and hit the target, but to distract.

With each bolt she released, she felt another presence touching her mind. She shook it off as she worked to help Marcus, but it wasn't worth it. Devan dodged each of her lightning attacks with awesome grace and control in the air while raining down blows on Marcus, who seemed to be ready to fall to his knees.

It was between two of her bolts that the angel landed a hit. He rolled in the air, folding his wings in, to just barely miss her attack, then dove behind Marcus, who was expecting another strike from above. Before Coura could shout a warning, Devan sunk his blade into the center of Marcus's back until it protruded from the front of his tunic.

"Marcus!" she screamed as the angel removed his blade slowly to savor the moment, and the soldier fell forward. Coura watched as his back grew red with blood.

What can I do? she thought weakly as Devan turned his attention to her. He wiped Marcus's blood off his sword onto his shirt with a sickening grin, making Coura's knees begin to shake. She wanted nothing more than to crumble onto her hands and knees and wait for death to come.

In her defeated state of mind, the growing presence from before seemed to take hold of her body, relaxing her frantic heartbeat and quivering body.

{*Use your sword now!*}

I don't have a sword!

The angel stalked toward her, and she began backing up.

{*Idiot! Remember the blade you used before?*}

A vision, clear as day, came to Coura. As she was near death against a tree with a sword in her chest, the memory returned of her removing the female angel's blade, letting it fall to the ground while blood trickled down her chest. She had ignored the irritating sensation and called forth a demon blade and wings, both black in color, without a thought.

How did I do that? she wondered instead of questioning the memory.

{*Don't you know anything? Call it forth as if you're casting a spell.*}

Coura felt a tingle of energy flowing from deep inside her core, beneath what she thought was the center of her power. It felt delicious, like drinking a sweet wine, and hummed in her veins, bringing with it a new sense of confidence.

Despite the angel only feet away, amid the sudden pounding on the metal door of the academy in the background, Coura closed her eyes and focused.

As if I'm casting a spell...

With a clear mind, she felt for that new energy, grabbed it, and imagined it manifesting in her hands. She could picture the blade, feel her power taking shape. When she opened her eyes, it didn't startle her to see the same sword from that night in her hands.

At first, Devan went wide-eyed with surprise and a hint of fear, probably at the memory of losing his foot. He reached down and rubbed his leg in confirmation, then stood up to glare at Coura.

"I feel it. That sword, that demonic energy doesn't belong in this world," he said, so serious she wondered what he was thinking. She was about ready to charge when the voice in her mind stopped her dead.

{*Don't expect to keep up with him without your wings.*}

My ... wings?

{*You are so helpless. Yes, your wings.*}

The utter lack of concern in the strange voice made Coura curious, but her thoughts were cut off by another sudden flashback.

This time, Coura was above the ground, leaping on the female angel and watching as her head rolled off her shoulders. Then, she turned to Devan and pumped her wings as if they were an extra pair of new limbs, throwing herself forward. She felt the air blow cool on her face, felt it on her wings beneath her tickling feathers too.

As the memory ended, she longed for that sensation again, of flight and freedom.

{*Do the same as with your blade.*}

She followed the voice's instruction and pulled from her center without closing her eyes this time. Devan sensed her energies and leapt back, instantly on guard.

"Demon," he seethed.

With a push of his wings, he flung himself at her, sword raised, but Coura was ready. She not only brought up her sword to meet Devan's but manifested her wings as soon as their blades touched, calling forth the spell. It cost her more energy than with the blade, but both spells fed from her center. Normally, she could feel when they drained her energy pool, yet this newfound power didn't seem to have a bottom. With exhilaration, she grinned up into Devan's face.

"You die here!" he shouted in response to her unexpected giddiness before jumping backward and into the air once more.

Without thinking, Coura leapt up after him, letting her wings pump her up to his level as naturally as running beside him. Devan initiated their fight by diving to strike, and she easily blocked it from below. Then, the two fell into a pattern of equally matched dodges and blows.

Coura managed to skirt away from and block each of the other's strikes. She swiped him across the chest, his left arm, and across the cheek. He swore each time and charged her frantically. While she enjoyed being in the sky, he seemed to become more frustrated as time passed by. Finally, after she nicked him on the chin, the angel descended to the ground and tried shooting flames up at her.

Unlike him, she wasn't used to aerial maneuvering. His first fireball hit her straight in her left wing, causing her to gasp from the unexpected pain and the wing to crumple. That was when she decided to move back down where she was used to fighting. Twice more, Devan's flames hit her, but with less of an impact than the first. Another tendril of energy flowed from her center to the spots where she had taken hits, but Coura was too focused to look into what it was.

Once on the ground together, the two continued trading blows while the distant pounding noise grew.

"Where's that ferocity and mercilessness you demonstrated before?" Devan yelled at her once he stepped back a few paces, separating them for the moment. He was panting with blood dripping into the grass in multiple places along his body. Coura's left wing dully ached, but otherwise she felt only a thrill.

When she didn't answer, he spat at her. "Demons don't belong in this world," he said with underlying resentment.

Coura glared at him and raised her sword. "This is your last chance. Leave this place or surrender and turn yourself in." The angel only brought his blade up again and stalked toward her.

{*We must end this quickly. Focus your attention on your sword. Put every bit of strength into a final killing blow.*}

I can't do that, Coura answered the voice in alarm. The thought of ending someone else's life was both horrifying and sickening, even if the person in front of her was crazy.

{*You are a mage. It is your responsibility to keep peace by any means necessary, right? Do you not think it is justifiable to kill in order to defend yourself? The strong should not show mercy to the weak. That is the way the world works, dear one. Besides, if you don't hurry, your friend over there is going to bleed to death.*}

Although Coura wasn't sure exactly what the voice meant, she trusted it as much as she could. Some other presence helped steady her hands as Devan charged, and somehow her breathing slowed enough to help her mind clear. When he was nearly upon her, Coura ignored his raised blade and swung her sword horizontally at his waist with full confidence. The angel turned his blade quickly to block the blow but wasn't prepared for her to risk her life by striking at the same time. His blade faltered as he tried to protect himself instead of following through with the attack. However, it was too slow to stop hers. Coura sliced through his midsection in one long motion without any restraint, stepped back, and waited with sword poised.

The angel took a wobbly step backward, then another, as he held his wound before falling onto his back, all while howling in pain before quieting. He remained unmoving, and Coura waited a moment until she was sure he was dead to relax.

Instead of the relief or nausea she expected after such an experience, she was still shuddering with excitement, taking pleasure in her newfound strength. It was Marcus's coughing that snapped her away from those emotions.

She cried out his name, sprinting to kneel at his side as dread and fear replaced everything else. He managed to flip himself over onto his back and pressed hands weakly against the wound.

200

Coura released the spell she held on her blade, causing it to disappear except for glimmering shards of energy that eventually faded, and placed both hands on top of his. His face was pale, and he grimaced at the extra pressure.

"H-how did you..." he began weakly.

When all of the strength and confidence she had moments ago fled, it left her shaking again. "I don't know," she said quickly, focusing completely on stopping the bleeding.

"What ... happened to..."

"I don't know, now stop talking!" she ordered as her mind raced. For what seemed like hours, Coura tried to think of what to do while on the verge of tears.

I did this, she thought with dread. *He would be fine if I hadn't been out here. I shouldn't have left! I ... I didn't mean to...*

Guilt wracked her then, enough to let several tears slip down her cheeks. The other presence in her mind didn't say anything, but she knew it watched.

14

A loud clang from nearby caught Coura's attention just as she began to give up hope. She watched as the damaged metal door leading into the academy creaked until whoever was behind it managed to push it open. Not only was Byron and the three trainees she sent inside present, but several instructors, the headmaster, and a lot of other students huddled behind. As soon as the door opened, everyone seemed to freeze in surprise at the sight of her and Marcus.

No, not Marcus...

That was when Coura realized she had yet to release the spell keeping her wings present, so they fell back behind her for everyone to see. When no one moved, she knew they were questioning whether or not to come forward, and she decided to call out to them.

"He needs a healer! Please, someone help him," Coura shouted, her voice nearly breaking.

One of the light mage instructors, Sylvia, shook her head as if snapping out of a spell, and ran forward. That seemed to be the signal for everyone else to go too. Two other light mages Coura did not recognize came forward to join the master mage. The older woman knelt on the other side of Marcus, careful to focus only on him. Coura removed her now blood-soaked hands while the woman replaced them with her own. The two other healers put theirs on top of the mage's, and she felt their light energies at work. Meanwhile, Byron hurried to Coura's side but didn't kneel like the rest.

"Will he be all right?" he asked the woman while eyeing Coura, who kept her face down at the ground.

"We'll see momentarily. It's a serious stab wound that literally put a hole in him, and he's lost a lot of blood. If it can be healed, we'll have to make sure the blood can be replaced. My students and I can handle this if that's what you're asking."

"Good," Byron nodded, and Coura felt his eyes on her again, remembering the blood coating her black feathers.

"I need another healer," he called to the group still waiting at the door. She kept her eyes on the ground.

{*Tell them not to bother. Your wounds are already healed.*}

It was a surprise to Coura, but after checking the tendrils of energy that reached out to those spots, she realized that while she had been fighting, that power had healed her injuries.

"I'm all right," she said loud enough for Byron to hear. Without so much as a thought, she released the spell for her wings, and they faded away, just like the sword, to many gasps and mumbles farther away.

With everything that had happened, Coura felt herself dropping into her thoughts and fears, and she probably would have continued if Byron hadn't grabbed her arm and hauled her to her feet. He made his way back to the entrance, dragging her behind, as she avoided meeting anyone's stare. Those near the door moved out of their way, either coming out into the grounds or pushing themselves flat against the walls inside. Without a word, and without looking at Coura or anyone, Byron pulled her through the door and into the eerily silent academy.

Once they were safe inside her room, he locked the door and pulled the curtain over the window. Without the extra energy and confidence, Coura had to sit on her bed to avoid her legs giving out. She couldn't meet his eyes, instead staring down at her clasped hands. The silence grew unsteady, and finally, she decided it was in her best interest to speak first.

"Byron, I'm sorry. I should've stayed inside, but I just—"

He raised a hand, signaling her to stop talking. When she was quiet again, he pulled over the chair from her desk and sat down with eyebrows knitted in thought. "I want to start from the beginning. Tell me about what happened after you brought me out of the tavern in Fester."

* * *

For the first time in her life, Coura felt completely exposed as she waited for Byron to process the story she recalled for him. Although her memories were restored, this was the first time she had followed them in order. The haunting images, descriptions of the demon-like power, horrific murders, intentional and not, made her feel terrible. In order to tell him everything, she had to distance herself from the girl in her story, to pretend it wasn't *her* but what she saw through someone else's eyes. What was worse, she constantly felt that other presence like another set of eyes in the back of her mind, silently observing.

She didn't know what to say or do outside of explaining her experience, the concrete facts of the past. Her thoughts were both racing to keep up and completely lost, leaving her unable to examine her own feelings and form her own judgement of the situation. Because of this, Coura chose to avoid including the voice who spoke to her and instructed her through the demonic powers.

Byron closed his eyes when she began, savoring every word. They didn't open until well after she concluded with the moment he and the others were able to open the door out to the magic grounds. He stared at the floor of her room for a long time with an unreadable expression.

Outside, she knew the sun was beginning to set by the light dimming from behind the curtain. With nothing else to say or do, Coura watched the light fade, her mind blank. Finally, when the room was dark and the silence grew too unbearable, she turned to Byron and prepared to ask his thoughts, only to find him watching her with interest.

"What?" she all but whispered.

Byron opened and closed his mouth twice before speaking. "I have many questions," he said very slowly, as if each word required careful consideration, "but the first I want to start with is... Are you OK?"

Coura blinked in surprise. "I ... don't know. I haven't had time to take it all in," she answered quietly.

Byron nodded as if he had expected that reply. "Then my next question is, what do you plan on doing now?"

"What do you mean?" she asked and tensed at his seriousness.

His body was as stiff as a statue, and there was no familiarity toward her in his eyes. *He's looking at me like I'm a complete stranger,* Coura thought with a sinking heart.

"I'm going to be honest with you," he began again. "This is bad. *Very* bad. Demonic possession usually results in a death penalty. It's unpredictable, and the risks associated with harboring someone that might snap are high. If you're not killed for that alone, there's the murder of two people, two angels."

"I didn't—" Coura interrupted before Byron cut her off.

"Not everyone will believe what you told me about it being out of your control. We didn't know their motives, and we never will now. Besides, there's still the matter of that demonic power." Byron paused as if waiting for Coura to respond, but she could only lower her eyes.

He's right. I can't defend myself when the country doesn't tolerate demons. There is no way to get around that fact, and what everyone out there saw.

"Now, I will ask you again. What do you plan on doing next?"

* * *

Byron watched his student with difficulty, trying not to give in to the urge to do one of two things. Firstly, he wanted to run to her, wrap her in his arms, and make sure she was physically and mentally all right. To have her not only in harm's way once but *twice* now under his watch was painful. Yes, he had past students assigned as soldiers and mages in the army, and some who died, but none he had spent as much time with as Coura. He was her guardian throughout this part of her life as she matured.

Secondly, he wanted strongly to place her under guard and make this room a prison of sorts until he was sure she was safe to be around. Her explanations didn't add up, based on his experience with demonic possessions, for three reasons. Very few who were possessed survived the initial reaction to how great the impact of demonic energy can be on the body. Those who did survive typically lost their minds once they returned to "normal." Each case he'd ever heard of ended with death, whether it was caused by another random surge of power or by order of the law.

For Coura to survive such power twice was a miracle, but there was always the possibility of another outburst. However, thanks to her returned memories, she said the first time she barely knew what was happening because she passed out from blood loss earlier. This second time she was in control of what was happening. How that was possible, Byron had no idea.

Lastly, and most concerning to him, were those wings. No demon was ever recorded to have wings like the angels'. It was blasphemous, yet Byron, and unfortunately too many others, saw them with their own eyes.

So, the question became what to do with Coura. There was no doubt the entire academy knew about what had happened. The only silver lining was that her story matched Will's completely. All this he thought about as she finished talking. Both sides of him were conflicted, yet his nature was to remain impartial. That was when he asked her what she wanted to do.

"You could either stay under close supervision with the *possibility* of the death penalty. We would question you tirelessly, and the whole academy would know. You'd become an outcast, Coura. Or you could run away. I wouldn't stop you if you opened the window and fled, but just know you will be hunted and presumed a traitor. You might have the best chance at surviving outside of these walls, though. The choice is yours."

"It's not much of a choice," Coura said with a tired sigh.

Byron remained silent and continued to watch for any movement, any *hint* of action that might set things off.

"I'd like ... to stay here," she finally said and met his eyes with new life.

* * *

Coura knew Byron's choices before he even laid them out. She had spent this little amount of time she had considering the outcome of her newly found power and ultimately decided she would be better off cooperating under his supervision. Not only that, but if she could show some control over herself, perhaps they wouldn't kill her after all.

As she stated her choice, Byron let out his own sigh of relief and looked at her with warm familiarity again. "I'm glad you're staying, but I will warn you it won't be easy. I don't just mean convincing everyone you're sane. There's still the matter of the angels and their intentions, especially since only you, Will, and Marcus interacted with them."

"I know. I'll take it all on," she said with growing determination.

Byron stared up at the ceiling in thought. "I'm going to have to ask you for a lot, Coura, so please be patient. I think I might be the only one who will be on your side in all of this. I don't want you acting irrationally. To be blunt, you're not exactly the most reasonable person to deal with." Only the small smile on Byron's lips told Coura he still considered her worth protecting.

That thought led her to another decision. "Byron," she began in a soft, uncomfortable tone, "There's ... something else I need to tell you."

{*Don't...*}

The lingering presence finally spoke up in a threatening tone. A shadow crept over Coura's body, and it felt as if there were an invisible hand at her throat. Byron, sensing a shift in the conversation, glanced at her with curiosity. *I have to tell him. He's more than just some man. He's my friend, and my mentor.*

After a moment, he shook his head and stood. "I don't want to hear it. Not yet anyway. You've given me enough to think about, and enough to work with. Besides, I think you could use some alone time to contemplate things."

What "things" Byron didn't mention, though Coura knew she had to form her own conclusions based on her decision to stay. "All right, so I should just stay here then?"

"Well, let's just say you won't have much choice for now," he said, knitting his brows together again in his serious tone.

"Fine. I'll wait for you, I guess."

"Good, and thank you. Also, don't be surprised if there are people guarding your door and window."

"I know, I know," Coura yawned and stood to stretch.

"I will have someone bring your meals here too. Once I know more, it'll be passed along."

Byron opened the door to see three young students carrying weapons, their backs to the door. They jumped in unison at his exit and tried to peek into the room. He ignored them and closed the door before Coura could catch their expressions or the conversation that was sure to take place.

Once alone, Coura couldn't help herself from pacing around the room in anxiousness as her thoughts continued stirring. *The last time I was alone was in the garden, before the angel came. I felt ... different than I do now. I know this feeling too. It was when I ... that night with Will ... and the other two.*

She glanced down at her hands, slightly shaking. *What am I? Am I possessed?* In that moment, Coura felt the presence in the back of her mind. *You, you're a demon, aren't you?* A tickle of amusement came from that corner where the voice was.

{*It's about time you started figuring things out.*}

"Who are you?" Coura spoke out loud and took a seat on her bed again.

{*You have much to learn, dear one.*}

"That doesn't answer my question," she grumbled. There was a pause as the demon-woman contemplated what she would tell Coura.

{*Ask me what you would like to know, and I will answer what I want you to hear.*}

That's not fair! Coura thought with frustration.

"Am I possessed? I mean, I know you're still inside me, but..." She hesitated.

{*Are you a danger to others?*}

Coura swallowed hard at the words she couldn't bear to ask.

{*It all depends on you. The choices you make, how you use our power, it will shape many things.*}

She laid herself down on the bed and stared up at the ceiling. "So, I won't randomly transform into a monster?"

{*Perhaps. If you don't let yourself get near death again, you should be fine.*}

Coura could hear the grin behind the demon's words. "OK, what now? How do I convince everyone I'm not some evil being that will hurt them?" The demon laughed, a crisp sound clear in Coura's mind.

{*What to do? I suppose you should learn some control over your new abilities. A human with power but no control is frightening and threatening. A human with control over their power is a lot more reasonable to deal with.*}

"You can teach me? How? Aren't you just a voice in my head?"

{*You forget you are talking to a pure-blooded demon. Remember how I guided you against that angel? It's similar to that. I am able to direct my energies and show you what to do.*}

"I see. That makes sense." Coura paused to consider everything the demon had said so far. "What should I call you? Can

I talk with you mind to mind? I'll look pretty crazy talking to myself all the time."

{*Idiot, you've spoken with me through your thoughts before. I can sense what you're thinking and feeling too, and my name is Soirée.*}

"Soirée..." The name felt wrong to say, like when she was a child using a curse word or first learning a spell, knowing the sound meant more than what was on the surface.

{*It seems we have quite some time to get acquainted in this sad, tiny room. Why don't we get started then?*}

Coura thought about the offer and recalled what she knew about demons. *They're tricky, and they like to cause humans pain. She's right, though, I need to learn control, and she's the only creature able to help. There's so much I have to do to prove myself to Byron and the others.*

Amid all of the nerves and strain, deep down Coura felt a flicker of that old thrill and a rightness about what she was doing.

Earlier, I was so concerned about staying here. I didn't know what to do with my future, and I wished for freedom. With these wings, I can go anywhere and see anything. Perhaps this change is destined. On the other hand, it might bring me harm and death.

She swallowed hard and forced a weak smile. "All I know is that this is going to be an odd, terrible story one day."

As a tremendous desire for something unknown to her flowed from Soirée, Coura wondered if she had made the right decision to trust the demon with her life.

About the Author

Courtney Lillard is a Wisconsin-bred "Writer for Fun" who takes pleasure in sharing stories that entertain readers, whether they are fantasy-fiction lovers or those trying something new. After living and traveling all over the Midwest, she is currently in Nebraska with her husband where she hopes to continue publishing the rest of The Dark Angel series and grow as an author.